# Running out of time

They sprinted through the immense cavern without a second glance at the awesome stalactites that hung suspended like stone icicles from the ceiling. The occasional sentry was caught in a stance of frozen surprise, then cut down by a hoarse burst of fire as he moved for his gun.

On the third level they found the room they were looking for. Billy Two fired his double-barreled shotgun, and a portion of the door splintered into fragments. Barrabas kicked it open. Huddled against the far wall was a man, his face white and fearful but resolute. It was David Young, the missing scientist.

"We're your rescuers," Barrabas shouted, and waved the man forward. "Let's go!"

The scientist frantically grabbed Barrabas's wrist and peered at his watch. "We won't make it. I timed the bomb to detonate in five or ten minutes."

"You what—" Barrabas started to say incredulously, but his words were cut short. From speakers hidden in the ceiling a piercing alarm sounded a long, steady wail.

## SOBs®
### SOLDIERS OF BARRABAS

SOBs®
SOLDIERS OF BARRABAS

THE BARRABAS
FALLOUT

JACK HILD

A GOLD EAGLE BOOK FROM
WORLDWIDE®

TORONTO • NEW YORK • LONDON • PARIS
AMSTERDAM • STOCKHOLM • HAMBURG
ATHENS • MILAN • TOKYO • SYDNEY

First edition January 1989

ISBN 0-373-61628-7

Special thanks and acknowledgment to
Jim Mandeville for his contribution to this work.

Printed in U.S.A.

## 1

In the countryside near Amarillo, Texas, it was the crack of dawn, sunrise barely a line of white at the far edge of the horizon. The old frame farmhouse four hundred yards across an open field was a silhouette of darkness.

The soldiers of Barrabas stood silently around a black van on a gravel road. For them it was the patient hour, the slow emptiness in the moments before battle. It was night enough yet for them to infiltrate invisibly. By the time they were in position the growing light would allow them to see.

Still, all the mercs shoved flares into their web belts, alongside the extra mags, concussion grenades, canisters of tear gas and sharpened knives.

In the back of the van, Nile Barrabas watched heat patterns on the monitor of an infrared sensor. Liam O'Toole and Claude Hayes were on either side of him. The redheaded Irish American peered over the big man's shoulder.

"To the right," Barrabas murmured quietly into a microphone.

Outside, Lee Hatton and Alex Nanos followed his instructions, slowly turning the barrel of the sensor to focus on another section of the farmhouse several hundred yards away.

The heat image of the building on the screen gradually changed. Claude Hayes, his skin shiny in the light from the monitor, tapped one of the several thickening red spots.

"Men sleeping in bedrooms," he said.

"There, and there." Barrabas's index finger touched two other dense areas of red on the screen.

"Plus one keeping guard along the driveway."

"All that I expected."

However, it was the existence of electronic sensors set in a one-hundred-yard radius around the farmhouse that created a problem for the mercs. It wasn't a sophisticated anti-intrusion system, but it was effective. As soon as one of the invisible beams was broken, by a person walking past, for example, alarms went off.

Hayes fingered another red spot on the screen. "Someone's on the second floor here, but in a room some distance from the others. That's got to be our missing scientist—"

"If he's still there," O'Toole interrupted with a dose of Irish cynicism. "It's too bloody easy to find him first time around.'

The scientist, Dr. David Young, had been kidnapped from the Federal Research Center at Los Alamos five days earlier. A young family man in his early thirties, he was one of America's foremost atomic physicists. There was no question who was behind his kidnapping, either.

Eight men, heavily armed and wearing green camouflage clothing, had killed six guards with automatic weapons at the gates of the research center just as Young drove in for a morning of work. They dragged the scientist kicking and screaming from his car. As more security police rushed toward the steel chatter of automatic gunfire, two of the kidnappers used M-79 grenade launchers. The explosions sent deadly shrapnel flying in wide arcs among the guards, killing twelve more, wounding eight.

The attackers fled in a black 4x4, leaving behind them the carnage of blood and dismembered limbs. The escape vehicle was found abandoned several hours later, but the identities of some of the kidnappers were no secret to federal authorities. Surveillance video cameras had recorded the entire event.

The kidnappers were part of a fanatical racist society known as the Aryan Nation, a home-brewed, midwestern amalgam of the Ku Klux Klan and American Nazi Party. As it turned out, the Feds had names, fingerprints and even mug shots of some of them.

Two of the men were fugitives from the law, wanted on murder and racketeering charges in several midwestern states. Ronald Doule, a massive heavy man with a black beard and dark hypnotic eyes, appeared to be directing the kidnapping. He was a known Aryan Nation leader, and had been on the run for more than a year.

Two other attackers were brothers, Duane and Keith Rotsky, also on the run from racketeering charges in Colorado and Washington State, as well as federal counterfeiting charges. They, too, were known members of the Aryan Nation. Keith Rotsky was also known as the Field Marshal, according to informants. FBI investigators theorized that Keith Rotsky had earned the name because he was responsible for much of the ruthless organization's terrorist strategy.

The other kidnappers remained unidentified. Several appeared to be young men whose faces were obscured by shadow or who were too far from the hidden video cameras to be clearly recognizable. One of them, a man identifiable only by his long blond hair, had taken the time before he fled to kill half a dozen wounded guards with a series of well-placed bullets shot into their heads execution style.

The cold-blooded killers disappeared with their kidnap victim, probably into an extensive underground network. The network had been set up by organizations along the lines of the Aryan Nation and with names such as the Posse Comitatus—Latin for Power of the County—and the Sword, the Covenant and the Arm of the Lord or the SCA.

The people in these groups were oddball survivalists, awaiting the imminent arrival of the end of the world, a great race war or some similar catastrophe. They were linked by a Christianity-based religion that held that white people should rule, while other races were "mud people." They had other equally strong convictions that were not open to being questioned by anybody, and because they believed these ideas so strongly, they were willing to kill for them.

They had safehouses and secret compounds throughout the midwestern states from Texas as far north as Idaho. Federal authorities knew the locations of some of these places, but arming themselves with search warrants would have been futile. It would simply have served to warn the perpetrators that the boys in blue were on their way. Worse, Aryan Nation and Posse Comitatus members had infiltrated the sheriff and court offices in dozens of counties.

So far, the kidnappers had not issued their demands for the return of the kidnapped scientist, but a dozen of their fellow travelers were currently serving life terms in a number of state penitentiaries. The ransom was expected to be a demand for their release. And those imprisoned were particularly bloodthirsty adherents. If Dr. Young was to be saved, time was of the essence.

Washington, or more properly, somebody from the NSA, called in the heavy guns—Nile Barrabas and his covert action team, the SOBs. They could circumvent the laws without a qualm.

As he stepped down from the stuffy claustrophobic van, Barrabas breathed greedily the fresh, faintly sweet air gusting along the flat Texas landscape. Shadows in shades of gray emerged from the dimness, showing the fence, the line of trees that formed a windbreak, the road leading past the house.

The other mercs waited outside. Lee Hatton, the sole woman on the team, and Alex "the Greek" Nanos maintained the infrared scanner positioned on the darkened farmhouse. Not far away, full-blooded Osage Indian Billy Two was a bear-size silhouette.

The mercs wore black camou suits stuffed tight over bulletproof vests and black steel-toed jackboots. Their faces were blackened. In the early half-light, they looked like aliens.

"Pack it up," Barrabas ordered quietly. He glanced at his chronometer. "We hit them in two minutes."

Quickly, Lee Hatton helped Nanos close up the scanner and put it in the van. O'Toole and Hayes gathered with the others.

Everyone knew where they were going and what they had to do. Each carried a silenced Magnum .22, a little gun that went *pop* in the night and shattered a man's skull as though it was a melon. For backup, they had Uzis strapped across their backs and spare mags in their web belts.

The Kevlar vests had been a trade-off: added weight and slightly less agility for some protection against bullets. In the end—and considering the possibility that they were going to be facing a hail of bullets on unfamiliar territory—the mercs had opted to wear them. But not without the reluctance of some members of the team.

"A man can get careless with his thinking when wearing one of these," Claude Hayes muttered, patting his hands up and down his padded clothing. "It shouldn't be like video games, y'know, where each player gets three chances before he's out. A man doesn't want to know he'd be dead if it hadn't been for this. It's tempting the fates. And it gets to be a habit."

Each of them also had a weapon that was a personal favorite stowed away somewhere. Barrabas liked his vintage Canadian-made Browning with its 13-round clip. Billy Two preferred the effective antipersonnel devastation wreaked by a .00-gauge double-barreled shotgun. Lee Hatton toyed with the blade of a shiny twelve-inch knife, twisting it back and forth in her hand. She was completely absorbed by it. The edge was razor thin.

Nanos watched, half curious and half amused. Lee looked up and saw him.

"I'm becoming quite good with a knife," she said softly, plunging the weapon into the sheath on her belt. And with a distant smile as she turned away, she added, her voice sounding almost seductive, "I've been practicing."

She floated to the front of the circle of commandos, on the side nearest the farmhouse, and stared into the dark shapes that filled the light. For a while after her lover, SOB airman Geoff Bishop, was killed, she had practiced with it, until she became obsessed and it occupied her to the point where it became a mania. Something else to think about other than grief.

By the time she was totally proficient, the impact of Geoff's death was beginning to lessen. She stopped knife throwing and got on with the rest of her life.

Barrabas watched the digital readout on his chronometer kick down the seconds. He could feel a readiness settle over him, the icy calm that came when every decision resulted in life or death. Theirs. Or his.

The chronometer read double zero.

"Billy Two!" Barrabas whispered. "Do it!"

The Osage moved, massive as a bear, and fell to his knees beside the fence. His hands moved quickly with the metal cutters, carving a large circle and pushing away the wire. He slipped through the hole.

He entered a border of small trees, barely as tall as a man. Billy Two towered over them. On the other side, an open field stretched four hundred yards to the house. Straight ahead, hardly fifty yards away, was the front gate to the ranch. One man stood guard. Crouching among the trees, the Indian headed straight for him.

He moved with the silence of wind as if his feet floated over the ground. All his senses led him toward his quarry, every nerve stretched taut and receptive to detecting any interference, anything unexpected, the least thing that was different from what it should be in the night.

The guard was in the road, just inside the wooden gate. He paced, grinding the gravel underfoot, and shuffling back and forth for warmth. He was tired and bored, which proved to be his last two mistakes.

Billy Two stopped in shadows, invisible, a predator waiting for the right moment. His arm swooped down, and his fingers connected with the hilt of his nine-inch knife like steel claws. Soundlessly the blade glided from the sheath.

In the east, the crack of dawn widened, and the white skin of the doomed guard's face and hands began to glow slightly in the still-thick gray of night. He was young. It was his last sunrise.

Some sixth sense must have finally alerted the guard, because he whirled around, his handgun drawn and probing the air wildly. He was just bearing down on the intruder when Billy Two pounced. His arms swung down, taking the guard's forehead in the palm of one hand, the knife in the other, and carving an arch through the skin and cartilage of his throat. The man's head flipped back like the lid on a box, gushing blood. Surprised eyes stared a frozen useless plea, as if life were an object beyond reach, disappearing ever farther into the invisible depths of dark waters. Billy Two saw life sink away and dropped the body.

The long low croak of a tired frog drifted from the nearby ditch. Overhead, wires strung along conductors on a pole snapped in the light gusts, buzzing and hissing with power surges.

Shadows moved on the other side of the gate, and Barrabas dropped into the compound, landing near Billy Two. The rest of the mercs quickly followed. O'Toole immediately began pressing plastic explosives onto the lock that held the gate closed.

"Remember," Barrabas whispered to the others, "the electronic movement detectors just inside the tree line."

There were silent nods all around. It was light enough now for them to just make out one another's features, and they made eye contact, then Barrabas tipped the needle nose of his silenced gun toward the farmhouse, motioning them on.

O'Toole stayed back to take care of the gate and transportation out. The other mercs loped silently up the road. The windbreak ended in fields that surrounded the house.

Approaching carefully, they dropped to their stomaches. Stubble from cut hay pressed against their faces. The mercs used their elbows and knees to crawl along the damp earth. The electronic sensors were placed on thin metal stakes two feet high. One of them poked up through grass several feet from Barrabas's nose.

Reaching the other side of the field, Alex Nanos leaped to his feet. The heel of his right boot skidded through wet mud and he slammed backward.

Inside the farmhouse, a hundred yards across the open field, a persistent alarm sounded, but it was inaudible to the encircling commandos outside. The men sleeping awakened instantly, reaching for weapons and clothing.

Claude Hayes grabbed Nanos's arm, and jerked the man to his feet. They had no way of knowing if the sensor had been triggered or not, but they also no longer had a choice. They were committed, even with the element of surprise gone.

Billy Two's chest heaved, and the eerie sound of a coyote chilled the dawn. The mercs took off, running all out and spreading in a line across the field.

Nanos and Billy Two spun off to the far sides and circled the back of the house. Barrabas led Hatton and Hayes to the front door. In the east, dawn widened to a rosy glow like the breast of a bluebird, bleeding away the cover of night.

Inside the house, men ran from their rooms, stuffing spare mags into their pockets as they went.

Barrabas leaped five steps onto the porch, silent as a cat. The front door opened from the inside. A bearded man stood in the opening three feet away, stark naked. He raised a rifle to his shoulder.

Barrabas's gun bucked once. The bullet coughed politely on its way through the silencer. The naked man smacked into a bullet, and his head disappeared in a spray of blood.

The mercenary leader dived to one side while Hayes and Hatton erupted through the door after him. The black man belted a mag out of the Uzi, raking the interior. Lee Hatton tossed a flare, which exploded into a pale flickering light. The commandos kicked past the body and burst through the doorway.

A tall man, also bearded, sprang from the stairs, leveling the short ugly snout of an Ingram MAC-10. Someone else dived from the interior darkness for Hayes.

Barrabas crashed into the man descending the staircase, knocking him against the railing. The torrent of bullets spewing from the submachine gun tore into the wall and ceiling behind Barrabas. Plaster exploded into a cloud of fragments and dust.

The man staggered sideways and the wooden railing gave way, the posts splintering and the banister crashing to the floor. He fell on his knees amid the debris, dragging the MAC-10 around. Barrabas shot-kicked to his face.

Boot connected to jawbone with violent force, and the attacker was tossed backward, head over heels. He crumpled in a heap against the wall, the whites of his eyes staring dully between half-closed lids. The gun was still held loosely in his limp hand.

"Way to go, Colonel!" Claude Hayes shouted from across the room. The black warrior slammed his fist into the face of the second attacker, spinning the man toward Barrabas. The mercenary leader lifted the gun and fired once.

The man's face was swallowed by a flood of crimson. He stopped, wavered on his feet and dropped like a stone. Without breaking his stride, Barrabas stepped across the lifeless heap. Dawn's weak early light streamed in the front door but failed to penetrate past the hallway. The rooms on both sides were dark and silent.

At the back of the house Alex Nanos smashed a window and leaped over the sill, sinking quickly to his haunches in a shower of splinters and broken glass. He twisted left, keeping his back to the wall. The big gun swung with him, clasped tightly in both hands and well out in front. His eyes tracked around the room.

An area of deep gray condensed slightly to a bare black shadow slinking stealthily across a doorway. Orange muzzle-flashes strobed the room, and a cascade of splinters exploded from the windowsill behind the Greek.

Nanos dived and somersaulted, coming up firing as fast as he could pump the trigger. There was a moment of stillness. The shadow leaned slowly across the doorway, and folded up quietly.

Still on the other side of the back door, Billy Two planted his foot squarely against the middle panel. He put his considerable mass of muscle and bone behind the kick, and like a coiled spring snapping at the knee, his foot punched forward. The hinges snapped from the frame and the door popped open, while the lock and handle, set in splinters of broken wood, held firmly to one side.

Starfoot raised his .00-gauge double-barreled shotgun and walked inside. He swept the area to his left the moment he went through the doorway. The blasts from the shotgun thundered in the confined space, and the muzzle-flash illuminated a kitchen, for a thin moment revealing a man who seemed to be barely upright, as if he was suspended for the briefest instant vertically. Most of the mass of his torso from his shoulders to his navel had been shredded against the wall behind him. The rest of him collapsed into a raw heap on the kitchen floor.

The kitchen was dark again, and Billy Two reached for a flare, simultaneously moving deeper into the house. Shots sounded from the front of the house and the next room, where Alex had come in the window.

The flare caught as the Osage moved farther into the house to rendezvous with Nanos and the other mercs. From above came the sound of feet stomping hurriedly across the floor of an upstairs room.

After coming in at the front of the house, Barrabas had moved left, while Claude Hayes and Lee Hatton fanned out to each side, deftly making their way by memory from the plans they had studied. The room now blazed with the sudden pink light from Billy Two's flare, just as the Osage's impressive shadow preceded him into the front room. Barrabas's dark silhouette was framed by the tender glow that filtered through the window behind him.

There was a crash at the top of the stairs and a harsh shout. Three men slammed into one another at the first step as they retreated in a panic. The one at the top raised his hands to shield his eyes. The other two looked for targets for their automatic rifles.

Two of them were found by bullets from the SOBs' weapons. One man's chest sprouted crimson blossoms from navel to throat. The projectiles kept on going after penetrating his body as if he was cardboard, and blasted into the man behind.

The first man spun about erratically, then thudded against the wall and tumbled slowly to the bottom step. His companion's feet were swept from under him as he collided with the bullets exiting his buddy's back. The force of his fall slammed him onto the steps, and he doubled over, clutching his stomach. Oddly, he sat up and looked with desperation at the mercs. Blood oozed from beneath his hands, and the look on his face said that he knew he was nearing the end, that the awesome moment was upon him. Death.

The third man retreated rapidly along an overhead hallway.

Hayes belted the silenced gun and leaped for the staircase. Pulling the Uzi into his hands, he rounded the corner at the top just as his quarry turned to fire. Lead slammed into the big black warrior's chest, four in rapid succession digging their way through the Kevlar vest and punching him backward with the force of a battering ram. He reeled, the air knocked out of him, and fought to catch his breath while tumbling down the stairs.

Barrabas flew past him, climbing three steps at a time and diving into the upper hallway near the floor with his Uzi on full auto. The fleeing man was caught by the hail of lead that slammed him against the wall and chomped chunks of flesh from crotch to neck. The dead man marked a bloody track on the wall as he slid down to the floor.

The merc leader paused to listen.

The house was silent.

"Nanos!" Barrabas shouted from the top of the stairs. "Billy Two. Up here!"

At the bottom of the staircase, Lee Hatton had quickly shouldered her rifle and gone to Hayes. She leaned over the stunned man. He tried a pained grin and began to push himself up.

"Goddamn, these things work!" Slowly he stood, taking in short agonizing breaths, and leaning carefully against the wall for support. His hand rubbed the scorched holes that ran in a line up his chest. The bullets were still there, trapped in layers of scorched cloth.

Hatton reached through the collar of the vest and felt his chest. "Bruised, but no ribs broken. If it wasn't for the Kevlar, you'd be dead."

Claude nodded grimly. "Ain't telling me nothing," he muttered, wincing as he rose to his feet. The pinkish glow from the flare flickered in a slight stray current of air, and fingers of light danced in corners and along walls. The room was littered with newspapers, magazines, empty beer cans and foam slabs thrown haphazardly around.

Hatton helped Hayes away from the stairs as Alex Nanos and Billy Two glided past them up the steps. On the second floor, they sank into darkness beside the colonel.

Four doors faced one another in pairs down a thirty-foot hall, which ended at a fifth. Daylight, pale and cold, filtered through a small curved window on one side of the hall. Somewhere downstairs, a door was battered back and forth by wind, clattering against the house with the jangle of broken glass.

The mercs moved forward. Barrabas and Billy Two took up position on either side of the hallway with their jackboots planted firmly against the doors. Their fingers tightened on the triggers. Barrabas gave a little nod. Their legs recoiled and pounded out like jackhammers, and simultaneously both doors burst inward. The mercs darted to each side of the door, their backs pressed against the wall.

There was only silence.

Barrabas groped for a flare on his web belt. It sputtered to life, and he tossed it around the corner, where it glared into a bright rosy light. He swung past the door, glancing inside and then flattening his back against the wall on the other side. The room was empty.

Alex Nanos followed the Colonel's example, and their eyes met across the hallway. The three men had taken up position against the other doors when Barrabas changed his mind. It was just a feeling, but something attracted him to the room at the end of the hall. He motioned to it, looking at Billy Two. The Osage nodded solemnly once and turned in that direction.

Suddenly the door burst wide open and a man jumped into the hall. With the pale light filtering through the window behind him, his features were shadowed, but the silhouette of light around him revealed his clenched hand pulling something away from his mouth.

Barrabas recognized the movement. "Grenade!" he yelled, throwing himself back against his men.

LIAM O'TOOLE FINISHED tamping the plastic explosives around the lock on the main gate, and pressed the detonator wires into the spongy material. He unrolled forty feet of wire and took cover behind a tree. Then he waited.

Slowly, the luminous second hand on O'Toole's watch swept around, and a minute ticked past, then two. It was almost time.

When gunfire erupted from the direction of the farmhouse, Liam O'Toole quickly triggered the detonator. A moment later a yellow explosion ripped at the gate, the thunderous boom echoing into the distance. Liam ran forward.

The gate was made of wood beams covered with sheets of galvanized iron. The explosion had only served to blow apart the lock that held it shut. The beams had broken, but the sheets of iron held the gate together. It swung freely back and forth in the slight breeze.

The black van was waiting in the ditch outside. O'Toole jumped in and started up. Keeping the lights out, he backed the vehicle, then turned onto the roadway that led to the embattled farmhouse.

THE MAN WITH THE GRENADE began to shriek something unintelligible. Barrabas, Nanos and Billy Two each ground home the trigger on his gun. A three-pronged stream of orange bullets shook the attacker like a rag doll.

The mercs dived headfirst for the stairs as the dead man sank to his knees and fell on top of the grenade.

The concussion wave of the blast swatted them forward, and the three mercs hit the landing on top of one another in a tangle of arms and legs. It was followed by a wave of gore, bits of bone and a warm wet rain of falling blood.

After the blast, the house was silent. The door downstairs began to flap in the wind again, banging against the house.

Nanos picked himself up. In the meager light, blood stained the walls and stairs around them. He looked over the top step. A lump of chewed flesh and severed limbs lay in a heap in the hallway.

"What a fuckin'—"

"Shht!" Barrabas hushed him quickly, raising his arm. With two big strides he regained the second floor and stepped over the carnage. Quietly, Nanos and Billy Two crept up behind him. The floor was slippery with blood.

They checked the fourth room. It was empty.

The sound of an approaching vehicle came from outside. O'Toole had arrived with the van. Then they could just make out another noise above the swishing wind and the creaking and moaning of the old frame house.

"A baby crying," Nanos whispered to Barrabas in disbelief.

It came from the room they had yet to check. Cautiously the three men crept forward. Nanos and Billy Two flattened themselves against the wall on one side. Barrabas let loose a kick at the door. It splintered and flew in, smacking against the wall.

They were greeted by the sight of women and children cowering near the open window.

"Shit!" Nanos cursed under his breath.

The three mercs stood in the doorway and stared in almost disbelieving silence at their cowering prisoners. Curtains at a window shimmered and moved in cool dawn breezes. Outside, the eastern horizon was aglow with sunrise, and an incandescent ball of gold floating on the horizon gazed on their waking nightmare. The pale white light that fell across the terrified faces was tinged with its carmine glow.

The two women were young, with long hair and plain faces. One held an infant, and wept, hiding her face. The second had pushed three other children behind her for protection. She stared at the mercs, her eyes flashing violent hatred, the ferocity of a mother defending her young.

The sound of the van approaching the house droned through the windows. It braked, and the engine idled. O'Toole was waiting. Barrabas checked his chronometer. In fifteen minutes state troopers and FBI agents would be crawling over the house. Time was up. "You won't be hurt," he said gruffly to the women, feeling sorry that they should be so misled and cast their lot with violent men led by hate.

Billy Two joined the surprised group after his search of the other rooms. "No scientist," he stated flatly.

"Leave them," Barrabas ordered gruffly, turning from the women and children. Anger flashed in his eyes, partly because of the involvement of innocent children and partly because of his frustration at the foiled mission. He motioned the mercs downstairs. "The FBI will be here in minutes. Let's get the hell out."

Like shadows cut from the fabric of darkness, the commandos raced from the farmhouse to the black van waiting outside. They had hardly piled inside when Liam O'Toole's foot hit the gas, and the mercenaries melted away in the dawn's pale light.

## 2

The long rambling ranch house sprawled along the side of a mountain, with the Utah foothills rolling from the distant highway to the front door. The barn and outbuildings also followed the line of the hill, so that from the highway the ranch looked like a fortress, its wooden walls the ramparts of the hills. A small cavalcade of vehicles, two Jeeps and a wrecker with a hydraulic winch, left the highway and moved up the road toward the house.

It was barely past sunrise, the same one that had greeted the carnage at the Texas farmhouse an hour earlier. In Utah, the countryside still had an undefiled air of fresh innocence.

A dog barked in the yard, and the sound floated across the silent distance. Then a human voice shouted. Something landed with a thud. The dog yelped and was silent.

Near the veranda and the front door a blue van idled. Three men stood nearby, smoking cigarettes and occasionally speaking softly. They chuckled and watched the mutt tied to a long rope near the back porch slink into the shadows with a series of pathetic whimpers.

After having hurled the piece of firewood at the dog to shut it up, Ronald Doule, Sr., went back inside the house and shut the door with an angry bang. He was a barrel-chested man of forty, with a huge black beard and hypnotic blue eyes. He wore his customary garb, a plaid shirt and jeans.

Doule, Sr., was the son of the deceased Wilbur Doule, a radical Mormon who had claimed, in his lifetime, to be a prophet of the church. On the lam for counterfeiting paper money, he had been killed in a shoot-out with federal agents eighteen years earlier, just after the birth of his grandson, Ronald Doule, Jr., known as Sonny.

Doule, Sr., had been in Vietnam at the time, a sergeant in the Air Cav. His tour of duty had been interrupted by his father's untimely and violent death—at least that was what most people understood.

In fact, it was a convenient excuse for a quick discharge. He had been found among a group of men running a black market in surplus weapons and ammunition, smuggling them to America sewn inside cadavers. There was no conviction by court martial for lack of evidence, but Ronald Doule, Sr., knew when it was time to quit.

He returned to Utah as the head of the family, the patriarch as it were, and quickly assumed his father's position as the leader of an organization known as the Aryan Nation. It had taken him those eighteen years to bring an old conspiracy to fruition.

Now was the time. So far, everything had gone off without a hitch.

The kitchen was bright with daylight pouring in the windows from the east. It was rustic, as was everything about the house. The floors were wooden, and the walls covered by faded wallpaper. A kerosene lamp glowed dimly on a sideboard, and a hand pump was beside the sink. A tall enamel pot on the stove hissed, giving off steam and the smell of coffee.

Three young men idled near the warmth of the wood heater beside the back door. Their weaponry—automatic rifles—stood at attention beside each of them.

Three women in long plain dresses milled back and forth at the counter. The largest one appeared to be the oldest. She had a pugnacious face and a wealth of graying hair that she wore in a loose mound on top of her head. As she moved from cabinet to stove to sink she watched the other two women work with the stern reproaching eyes of a supervisor.

A telephone rang, breaking the peaceful tranquility of the newborn day. The four men who stood around the room turned to look at Doule, wondering who was calling. From outside, the sound of vehicles in the distance grew louder as they approached.

"Coffee, women!" Ronald Doule snapped. "For everyone, and on the double."

All three turned. Bathsheba Doule, the older woman, was his mother. The two younger dark-haired women were his wives. Muriel was plain-faced and pimpled, although she was in her early twenties. Nora was the beautiful one. The one Bathsheba hated the most.

Ronald Doule, Sr., was determined not to put up with anything from his wives, not after having witnessed what his father had to put up with while married to Bathsheba. He expected complete submission and total obedience from both Nora and Muriel. Wife number three, he intended to add soon.

Ronald Doule strode into the next room and grabbed the telephone.

Nora wrapped a dish towel around her hand and reached for the percolator. The bubbling coffee hissed and settled in the pot. She laid out cheap glass mugs on the counter and poured a steaming stream of dark liquid into each.

Her husband's voice, murmuring into the telephone, floated in from the next room.

She handed a mug to each of the men in turn.

Gerry "Spiker" Chandler, a stocky broad-shouldered eighteen-year-old of medium height, stood by the kitchen window, occasionally tucking the curtains aside to peer outside.

A thin bony man in drab olive fatigues lounged against the wall near the stove. He was Peter Wrathe, and the proud possessor of the Chuka, from the sound he made when he pretended to kill people without pressing the trigger of his pretty tin MAC-10.

The third man, who waited quietly until last for his cup of coffee, was the outsider. Roger Wilco was a city boy. An enthusiast of Nazi memorabilia from a very early age, Wilco became a skinhead. He shaved his head and wore a black leather jacket covered with studs, high black boots laced tightly over his ankles and rolled-up black denim jeans. He looked out of place in the rustic kitchen, but he had much in common with the others.

He believed that scum came in all colors except white, and had to be eliminated. He had become an expert in jiu-jitsu, and various esoteric kinds of street fighting, like his favorite, using a bicycle chain. It was a weapon that in a city was virtually always available. He carried one now, stuffed through the epaulet on the right shoulder of his leather jacket.

Wilco had first heard about the Aryan Nation and the Posse on a television broadcast, when a number of members were sentenced to life imprisonment for murder and racketeering. As the anchorman spoke, Wilco had found himself nodding in agreement with the stated principles of the racist organizations. It took him two months to find his way inside. Now he was really going to do something about all the sick stupid lowlife that threatened America from within. He clutched his MAC-10 gleefully. He was going to kill them. It was neat.

There were footsteps on the porch outside.

Nora set down the coffeepot and turned when a tall young man with long blond hair opened the back door and walked into the room. Although only eighteen, he moved with the grace of a tiger when stalking prey. He was Ronald Doule, Jr.—known to the world as Sonny.

"They're here!" Sonny Doule addressed the room. His face beamed with anticipation. His eyes swept across the room, stopping briefly at Nora. It did not escape Bathsheba's attention that the young woman—her son's most recent wife—had met Sonny's gaze straight on for a barely noticeable fraction of a second. Bathsheba was convinced the woman was a harlot.

Around the room, the men stirred and reached for their guns.

"Who's on the phone?" Sonny directed the question at his grandmother.

At that moment, his father's voice in the other room stopped, and Doule, Sr., stepped back into the kitchen, his face dark, his eyes spitting sparks. With one hand he stroked his thick black beard over and over. Bathsheba turned away from the counter and walked toward him. She stood with her hands firmly planted on her hips.

The patriarch looked at his son and mother while his two wives continued to prepare food, casting furtive, surreptitious glances at their husband from time to time.

Sonny was the son of his father's first wife, a woman who had died after childbirth eighteen years ago. Doule was proud of him. As far as he was concerned, the boy could do no wrong. Sonny was a real sovereign—his son's birth had never been legally registered, and he had never attended school. The state had no knowledge of Sonny's existence—nor of the existence of hundreds of other young sovereigns scattered in Aryan Nation compounds throughout the Midwest.

Sonny had taken to the Aryan Nation struggle with the ease of a natural. Doule, Sr., pursed his lips. Almost too easily. There was a blood lust to the way his young son carried out orders. He remembered what Sonny had done to a turncoat named Willis, when they discovered the man was leaking information to federal investigators.

Sonny, Chuka, Spiker and Wilco had picked Willis up at his apartment, bound his hands and feet with tape and took him to the trash compactor behind a Family-Fun Steak House franchise in Denver. Spiker disconnected the safety switch that prevented the compactor from operating when the door was open. Before they threw Willis in alive, Sonny removed the tape from the doomed man's mouth, legs and hands.

Willis's begging and pleading was useless.

The desperate man was put into the compactor feet-first, like a pencil shoved into a sharpener. Willis let out horrendous earsplitting screams for a few seconds, while the machine devoured him with great shuddering gulps. The screams stopped when the gnashing blades reached Willis's groin. Then it was over. The fun finished, Sonny pushed the upper half of Willis inside and closed the door.

And Doule, Sr., remembered what his son had done during the kidnapping of the scientist in Los Alamos. Before fleeing, the young man had efficiently executed half a dozen of the guards with single point-blank shots to their temples. Sonny's methods were ruthless, but nonetheless efficient for the work they had ahead of them.

"The feds raided the safehouse near Amarillo," Doule, Sr., told the people gathered in the kitchen. "Duane Rotsky, all the men were killed."

"And the women and children?" Bathsheba demanded sharply, unable to conceal the horror on her face.

"The women have been arrested. The children have been kidnapped by the state."

Sonny Doule stepped forward, looking fiercely at his father. "Then we add their release to our demands!"

Doule, Sr., looked at his son carefully, silent for a moment, stroking his beard. "No," he said finally, with the authority of a pronouncement. "Not yet. We have far more important things to do."

Doule, Sr., walked up to Sonny and placed his hands on the young man's shoulders. "Be ruthless," the patriarch said, knowing the kind of ruthlessness that his son was capable of dishing out. "Show no mercy. Your objective is to get the material we need at the Webber Tunnel tomorrow and get it to Arkansas two days from now. Nothing else. Do anything you have to, to get it there."

Bathsheba walked over and took her grandson's hand. "Remember you are still a sovereign," she told him. She stepped back, addressing Chandler and Chuka, who were also sovereigns. Pointedly, she ignored the outsider, Roger Wilco.

"Remember that it has been revealed to us that we will found the new Aryan Nation, God-fearing, Christian and racially pure, freed of the yoke of government." Bathsheba's voice rose, and she waved her hand in the air with the gestures of an orator.

"It is written in the Bible that America is God's promised land, and that white people are the Chosen. The great war between the races is dawning! You are the soldiers of Armageddon. This is the second American revolution!"

She moved forward and reverently touched her grandson's face. "Sonny. Avenge these deaths." She brandished her fist. "In Texas, your uncle murdered. Your brothers and their wives. Avenge them. For all of us."

The young sovereign leaned forward and kissed Bathsheba Doule on the cheek. "I promise, Grandmother."

The men exited from the house just as the Jeeps and the wrecker rolled to a stop outside, close to the blue van at the foot of the steps. The other Jeep pulled in behind. The men in the vehicles greeted one another. Spiker Chandler slid back the side door of the blue van and went inside. Chuka walked around and climbed behind the wheel.

The Doules, father and son, stood on the porch to say farewell.

"What about Roger Wilco?" Sonny whispered to his father.

"What about him?"

"He's a fool. He can't carry his weight. He gets excited, he might blow something. He's a city slicker out for a good time. A loose cannon."

"He's a good fighter. He conducted himself well during the kidnapping."

"Yeah, but we had to make him carry a submachine gun instead of that damned bicycle chain he learned how to use on the streets of Minneapolis," Sonny grimaced. "He's got Spiker carrying a bicycle chain now, too. Sure, it's a great weapon for street fighting with punk gangs, but we ain't involved in that kind of stuff." He patted his coat, where the cloth revealed the compact outline of his MAC-10. "No matter what, when you face the Feds, this is more efficient."

His father's instructions were curt. "If Wilco gets to be a liability, get rid of him. We have no room for mistakes."

The two men looked at each other with an intimate understanding of what Doule, Sr.'s instructions meant. Once again, the bearded patriarch remembered what his son had done to the unfortunate Eddy Willis. The dead man had been a member of the Aryan Nation for several years before he decided to quit. Unfortunately there was only one way out after full-fledged membership.

"Bones in, bones out." Sonny slapped his father on the back, and left his arm there for a moment. The phrase was a code among the white supremacists. It meant that one has killed to become a member, and must die to be released.

"Bones in, bones out," his father replied. "Good luck today. And I'll see you in Arkansas in two days." The father slapped his son on the back.

His son nodded, pushed past him and went down the steps toward his waiting comrades.

AT THE FARMHOUSE IN TEXAS, the bloody dawn became a pleasant summer day. The air was dry and hot, but perpetually moving breezes swept over the wide open rangeland that spread to the horizon on every side. Along the narrow country road and around the farmhouse, the trees that had been planted as windbreaks tossed listlessly in the warm air currents that didn't cool the withering heat.

A dark blue Oldsmobile, the tinted windows sealed against the heat, pushed through a throng of reporters and television cameras jostling and demanding entry at the gate. The driver flashed his FBI credentials to the state troopers who stood guard, and the car was waved through.

Inside the air-conditioned vehicle, an immensely fat man in a gray suit reclined on the soft cushions. Walker "the Fixer" Jessup carefully observed the rows of troopers that lined the road or searched for evidence through fields of stubble and grass.

It was all a charade for public and media edification. Jessup knew that. Claymore Jeffries, the FBI director who sat on the seat beside him, also knew it. But the investigators doing the searching and the hordes thronging at the gate didn't. It was an important part of the plan.

The Aryan Nation, the Posse Comitatus, the SCA and the Christian Identity church had all disseminated a creed of hate that had spread among disaffected farmers from Texas and Arkansas to Iowa and Utah and into the Pacific Northwest. The rightful government of the United States was their sworn enemy.

Aryan Nation and Posse people had been responsible for bank robberies, train robberies and the wanton murder of state troopers and federal agents. Dr. Young was their first kidnap victim—and their first scientist.

One of the problems in tracking down the kidnappers was local cooperation. No one knew if local sheriffs could be trusted, or if they were Posse sympathizers.

There was also a matter of time. All the Posse and Aryan Nations members were known to be extremely well-armed and dangerous. An FBI raid on one house could cost lives or turn into a siege that lasted days. One way or another, Young would be dead before it was over. And the brilliant Los Alamos physicist's brain, crammed with invaluable knowledge about American nuclear research, was vital for national security.

Last, and by no means least, there was the matter of legality. A congressional member of the secret House Committee made Walker Jessup an offer. The FBI was to supply the location of Aryan Nation and Posse safehouses, where the scientist might be held. Jessup was to arrange for someone to raid them—quickly and efficiently, outside the law.

Jessup in turn turned to the man he had used many times before—ex-Special Forces colonel and Vietnam veteran Nile Barrabas, now a mercenary, and his highly skilled group of free-lance commandos. Barrabas was not a run-of-the-mill mercenary: his sense of right and wrong had heightened during the Vietnam experience, and his loyalty was unquestionable.

Barrabas was to take his people into the safehouses, one by one, using whatever means necessary. They were to ascertain if the scientist was present or not, free him if he was there and depart within a specified time frame. The FBI and local police would be "tipped" and arrive on their heels.

After agreeing on their usual fee of a quarter million dollars apiece, the Soldiers of Barrabas, better known as the SOBs, took on the mission.

In the back seat of the dark blue Olds, the Fixer sighed, and turned away from the landscape of his native Texas to talk to Claymore Jeffries.

Jeffries was in his forties and wore a crumpled blue suit that did little to conceal the shoulder holster under his left arm. His once handsome face was harshly lined by too many years of police work. He was the man Washington had sent to work with Jessup—the only man outside the special group known as the House Committee and the White House who knew what was really going on.

"You didn't tell us there were going to be women and children in there." Jessup ended his complaint with a slight shake of his head and turned back to the window. Barrabas hadn't been too happy about the women and children when he stumbled across them several hours earlier.

"Walker, we didn't know and we still don't know what they were doing here," Jeffries replied. "Our understanding was that the property was nothing more than a Posse Comitatus safehouse, used by some of their killers."

"Do we know who they are?"

"The wives and children of Duane Rotsky, the guy who ate the grenade. These people have some strange habits—like having more than one wife at the same time."

"Wives? Yeah, right. This cult," Jessup said slowly, "they believe in polygamy."

"Yeah, but get this. Rotsky's brother is known as the Field Marshal. He's a biggy in the Aryan Nation organization. Right-hand man to head honcho Ronald Doule himself."

Jessup's car turned off the road into the yard in front of the house. It was teeming with cars boasting side panel emblems for every species of law enforcement agency in the country. Ambulance attendants in white efficiently wheeled gurneys from the house, each with a single zipped-up body bag strapped to it.

At higher levels of state government, the upper echelon of the FBI and the Texas state troopers frequently argued about who had jurisdiction. The general lack of agreement meant that everyone at this scene milled around in confusion.

The county sheriff had sent his deputies in to start the cleanup, even before the FBI got there. In the house they'd found Aryan Nation literature, as well as a cache of automatic weapons, many of which were modified with silencers, dumdum bullets or vital parts filed down to make semis into full autos. But FBI specialists were concerned that evidence had been destroyed by the county sheriff's marauding deputies before the Feds even arrived.

"From what my people tell me, the women have been yelling that Rotsky's going to rise from the dead in some kind of holy resurrection, and then he's going to get us all," Jeffries went on.

"Hallelujah," Jessup muttered without enthusiasm.

The dark blue Oldsmobile rolled to a stop beside the steps leading onto the front porch. The cool antiseptic air in the car had been a soothing respite from the hot rays of the Texas sun. When Walker Jessup and Claymore Jeffries stepped outside, dry heat enveloped them. It was already ninety-six degrees.

Nearby, two women, a baby and three children sat on metal benches in the open back of a paddy wagon, guarded by a stern prison matron who had been brought out from the Amarillo police department. They looked quiet and docile, except for sniffling and the occasional choked sob. The children buried their faces against their mothers' bodies in fear. The women's eyes were dark, their faces suffused with hatred. They clutched their children protectively.

"A mighty poor sight," Jessup remarked and shook his head sadly.

The Fixer had once been a CIA operative, one of the best to go through Saigon's initiation by fire, from the 1968 Tet offensive to the flight from the American embassy in 1975. That was where he met the colonel the first time, too, Nile Barrabas, the man who turned out to be the last American to leave Vietnam, just managing to grab the skid as the last chopper lifted from the roof of the besieged Saigon embassy.

After the war Jessup went into the private sphere as a so-called security consultant. In fact, after two decades of CIA-sponsored espionage work in foreign lands, Walker Jessup had compiled an overfilled Rolodex listing names, addresses and favors owed. With that, he soon developed a reputation for fixing things—from the change of government in a Third World country to quietly smuggling nuclear secrets out of Pakistan or into Israel.

Little had he suspected back in the days of Nam that the famous white-haired colonel, the war hero who turned down his Congressional Medal of Honor, would someday be in his employ—although *employ* wasn't quite the right word.

The United States Government was the principal contractor, but Barrabas was his own man. He got to do the jobs his way, and so far, he and his people had proved themselves one hundred percent reliable.

There had been more than two dozen assignments for Barrabas and the team of ex-soldiers the Fixer had put together. Quite a few of the original group had died, and a couple of comrades were retired. But in terms of missions accomplished, the SOBs were still batting one hundred.

It was good work, and it had made all of them wealthy. On the other hand, if anything went wrong, Uncle Sam was going to throw his arms wide and plead total ignorance of the illegal activities of a group of mercenaries whom they knew nothing about.

Walker Jessup ambled toward the front door, finding his massive weight a disadvantage in the heat. He paused to wipe sweat from his forehead, when suddenly a chrome, phallic-shaped object was shoved into his face and a shrill voice demanded, "Mr. Walker Jessup! Fancy finding you here! How about giving me your comments on what happened...?"

Bill Stead, the anchorman for a nationally syndicated television current affairs program, stood before him. It was not the first time the Fixer had encountered him—both men were well known on the Washington cocktail circuit.

Jessup sighed with exasperation. A cameraman hovered in the background, his camera veering in on Jeffries and Jessup. They turned their back to him. The keen, fresh-faced television newsman quickly whirled around to confront them again.

"Bill Stead, *Report on Facts*, broadcast daily from coast to coast." The journalist smiled ingratiatingly. "Maybe you've seen my show?"

He was being facetious.

"You tell the guy with the camera to fade out, and we'll talk," Jessup yelled, swinging around once again to avoid the glassy eye of the camera. Stead thought for a moment, then waved the cameraman off. The man lowered the camera, sputtering in protest. Stead waved his hand. The cameraman traipsed off, disappointed.

"What in hell are you doing in Texas," Claymore demanded, "and who let you past the gate?"

The newsman appeared unperturbed. "Hey, it's your job to put guards around to keep me out, and it's my job to get past them. I'm just a humble reporter seeking the truth about the Aryan Nation for a special hour-long prime-time newscast. People are interested all of a sudden. Especially since nuclear scientists have started disappearing. Now, how 'bout it? What's going on, Jessup? Guys like you don't crawl out of the woodwork unless there's a bone to gnaw on. Do I get an interview? Or just the inside dope."

Jessup looked at the diminutive newsman with intense loathing. Jeffries stepped in, the standard and well-rehearsed media reply at the tip of his tongue.

As far as Jeffries was concerned, local law enforcement people and media could invent any explanation they wanted for the mess the SOBs left behind. Since the kidnapping had been publicized and there was video evidence that the Aryan Nation was responsible, Claymore's office in Washington carefully encouraged rumors that didn't involve the covert action team known as the SOBs.

"This bloody nighttime raid was probably the result of a power struggle among different factions of the Aryan Nation," Jeffries told Stead. As he spoke he raised an arm and signaled to several agents standing nearby. "Fallout from the kidnapping of the scientist, probably. That's all."

Stead snickered. "Thanks, guys. But everyone already knows that. I mean real inside dope. Something everyone doesn't know. Like, is it true that one of the bodies carried out of that house belonged to Duane Rotsky? And is Ronald Doule involved? And what is Walker 'the Fixer' Jessup doing here?"

Suddenly three FBI agents surrounded Stead. Jeffries smiled and glanced at Jessup while he signaled again to his men.

"Show Mr. Stead to the gate, please."

Squawking and protesting, the belligerent anchorman was hustled toward the road.

Jessup and Jeffries turned away and climbed the steps to the front porch. They walked into the house.

Out of the brutal rays of the hot summer sun, there was an immediate but short-lived sensation of coolness, but any relief was quickly dispelled by the scene that greeted them. No one had cleaned up the gruesome patches of dried blood and spattered flesh that had sprayed over the walls and floor. There was a bad metallic odor, and the great splotches of blackening blood buzzed with feasting flies.

"My God, the carnage!" Claymore Jeffries recoiled, clearly shocked.

FBI agents combed each room, looking for more information on the elusive fanatics who had just been knocked out. A big-bellied man, the county sheriff, strode through the front door and waved at them. He was out of uniform, wearing a loud, checkered sport jacket over the upper half of his short squat frame, and plaid pants below. The sheriff had been a particular thorn in the FBI's side.

"Someone stirred up a real hornets' nest last night," he drawled, turning from Jeffries to Jessup. His face split in two with a wide smile. Silver fillings flashed in a field of snow-white teeth. "And who might you be?" he asked with a shrewd look at Jessup. He looked like a shark.

Jeffries interrupted. "He's FBI. From the Washington office. Flew down when all this missing scientist business got started." He nodded to Jessup. "Gerald Jones, county sheriff."

The sheriff tilted his head doubtfully and looked Jessup and the agent up and down.

"They were surprised while asleep, judging from their partial dress," he said slowly. His back teeth ground down and he popped chewing gum. "Coroner says it happened about three hours ago. Right at the crack of dawn.

"Now, some of those reporters out there—" the sheriff jerked his head in the direction of the road "—they're asking me if this is an Aryan Nation place, and if they might've come in here and killed some of their own men in some kind of power play. I wonder where they got that idea. We don't have Aryan Nation types in this here county. I know for a fact they didn't do it. And all you federal agents invading my territory got no right to be here."

"Says who?" Jeffries snapped back. "You?" He turned around, ignoring the man. The sheriff's face reddened with fury.

Unhurried, Jessup and Jeffries sauntered to the front porch, leaving the house to the detectives. The air outside, though hot, was less polluted by the stench of death. Sheriff Jones stormed after them.

They were interrupted on the porch by a young FBI agent, who approached carrying a notebook and several plastic bags.

"Inspector Jeffries. We've been over the house once, and I have some preliminary results...." He held up the plastic bag filled with evidence. On top were several small bags filled with empty shell casings.

"By matching bullets with guns that aren't here, we know the attackers used a variety of weapons, including Uzis." He held up another bag. It contained a pair of spectacles. Jessup and Jeffries recognized them immediately. The county sheriff popped his gum at the back of his mouth.

"They aren't positively ID'd, but we're pretty sure they were Young's."

The FBI inspector turned to Sheriff Jones. "There's our proof. The kidnappers have crossed an interstate line. Now it's a federal case."

"Bah," the sheriff grunted. "You got no evidence that this is connected with that scientist kidnapped from Los Alamos. You don't even have evidence to show that an interstate crime was committed here, and as far as I'm concerned I'm in charge. I tell you—"

"Sheriff," Jeffries interrupted. "Butt out. That includes your men, too."

A car with state troopers' markings pulled up in front of the house. A man jumped from it and yelled to the big-bellied Texan sheriff. Jones acknowledged the shout and turned to the two men from Washington. He flashed a false grin under malevolent eyes and jerked his thumb at the door of the house.

"You gonna need a lot more than a pair of someone's spectacles to make your case. I tell you, this is nothing more than some feud among relatives, and one of them went blood simple. Before this day's out, we'll find some crazy brother-in-law or someone hiding out somewhere. If he hasn't put a bullet in his own brain already."

He looked defiantly at Jeffries. "Now I don't want you fellas to be in the way, so I'd be mighty pleased if you could round up your agents and make tracks."

He shuffled down the steps toward the deputy from the car, who walked across the yard to meet him.

The young FBI agent looked at Jeffries. "A fun guy," he commented, staring at Jones's receding backside.

"What did you get out of the women?" Jeffries asked him.

"The women won't talk but we got something out of one of the children, sir. The little girl. I showed her the glasses and asked her where they came from. She said another man lived in the house with them for a few days. I showed her a picture of Dr. Young and she ID'd him. She was a little vague on when it was, though. But he could have been taken from here as late as yesterday."

Jessup and Jeffries exchanged glances. They had missed, probably by a few hours. Undoubtedly the scientist had been moved to another safehouse. It meant the SOBs would be working again that night, and another strange shoot-out would hit the morning papers.

"Should we close up shop, sir?" the FBI agent asked Jeffries.

The senior agent shook his head emphatically. "The moment the sheriff comes armed with a court order telling us to get out, we get out. Otherwise, we stay put."

Jeffries and Jessup walked back to the Oldsmobile and gratefully entered the air-conditioned coolness.

"We just missed him," Jessup hissed, patting his sweat-drenched face with a damp handkerchief. Big wet perspiration stains spread from the sleeves of his suit jacket.

Jeffries glanced sideways at the fat man. "Getting your people to go in was the only way. But other enforcement agencies, and even my own men are starting theories about what's happening. If your people hit another Aryan Nation house tonight—"

Jessup put his hand up. "Look, it's the only way. First, we don't have to waste time with legal niceties. And if other law enforcement agencies and media people—especially a news hound like Bill Stead back there at the gate—if they think it's a homicidal maniac or warring factions of the Aryan Nation, they'll be thrown off the trail and won't be in our way."

The Fixer glanced at his watch. "Looks like they'll be due in Arkansas tonight. There's an isolated compound there that's next on our list."

Someone rapped on the tinted window. Jessup's pudgy finger hit the button on the door, and the window descended with a hum. It was Sheriff Jones. His jaw moved from side to side as his teeth worried the chewing gum. It popped, and his smile flashed silver teeth.

"Looks like it don't matter who's in charge no more," Jones drawled. "I just got the word on my car radio. They found your scientist. In a trash compactor in Albuquerque. Wasn't much left of him, from the radio report. Identified whose remains they were from a few teeth that didn't get ground up."

His lips returned to a leering smile. "Looks like you boys are out of your jurisdiction, after all. I'd appreciate it might good if you'd clear off and leave this here local business up to me."

## 3

It made him itchy under the skin. Barrabas didn't want to be in Wyoming, but he came anyway, as he always did once a year or so. Green River. With little more than the weather-beaten farmhouse he grew up in smack-dab in the middle of a section of the finest windswept grazing land in the state. It was a place he'd left with relief when, at the age of seventeen, the young Barrabas had boarded a bus in Cheyenne that took him straight to the Army recruiting station in Times Square, New York City.

Since then he'd seen oceans and cities, continents, wars and women, but no matter in what romantic light some people saw him Barrabas's origins could always be traced back to the small spread where he'd been raised. The romance of distant places was the lure that had drawn him as a young man, but it startled Barrabas how he had to remind himself of that from time to time. For a moment his mind flashed back across those years and all the roads he'd traveled, almost always heavily armed. And all the battles. But few, he thought, surprised him more than the one he'd fought in Texas barely a few hours before. It was unexpectedly finding the innocent children that still bothered him.

Living as a mercenary from day to day was a lot different from the romantic notions he'd had as a gung-ho kid. Barrabas resigned himself to what he was. A professional, with a job to do, and one he did extraordinarily well. Soldier for hire. Paid to make decisions and bring results. There were a lot of creeps out there, the kind that were so diabolical there could be no doubt that their annihilation was to the betterment of humankind.

The ones who'd taken the nuclear scientist were a case in point.

While he and his soldiers were raiding the Amarillo farmhouse, the Albuquerque police had received an anonymous telephone tip that directed them to the Ventura Restaurant, a big glitzy place with glass walls and plastic chandeliers. It seated fifteen hundred people. According to the last employee who left, at approximately 3:00 a.m., the trash compactor was empty and the gate was locked.

By the time the police arrived at six o'clock, the lock had been smashed, and the compactor was filled with ground-up human flesh. The powerful metal teeth had even crushed the thick thigh and pelvic bones. Only a few molars remained to identify the human being it once had been.

And according to dental X rays, the teeth belonged to Dr. Young, the missing scientist.

It was suspected that he had been killed before going into the compactor, perhaps by accident during the kidnapping. That would explain why his kidnappers disposed of his body without ever making their demands known.

Dr. David Young had been a family man, guilty only of having a career as a nuclear physicist at a federal research center. He was valuable to the government for his research on strategic missiles.

With the knowledge of Young's death, the SOBs to a man were ready to track down Duane Rotsky's friends, the perpetrators, the murderers, and bring them to justice.

Several things bothered Barrabas about the case. No one would have known the scientist's fate for days—if ever, and that would have given the kidnappers lots of time to extort something out of someone. Or to prudently disappear from sight. So why the telephone tip about the trash compactor?

And there was the matter of the video surveillance cameras that had recorded the whole kidnapping in blazing Technicolor. The kidnappers, mowing down a dozen guards with submachine guns at the gates of the Los Alamos research center, were too smart not to have taken out the cameras. It was as if they wanted the world to see them do it, on the seven o'clock news.

Barrabas and his soldiers were ready to keep going, busting up Aryan Nation safehouses until they found the culprits and dealt them the kind of homespun lynching justice they recognized.

Instead, word from on high stopped them. The SOBs were called off. One White House aide had even implied to Walker Jessup that the SOBs were responsible for precipitating Young's death by their violent actions. Attitude, not gratitude. That was what the mercs got from the government for risking their lives to do a dangerous job. Barrabas was kind of used to it. It wasn't the first time, and it wouldn't be the last.

Washington would come calling again when they needed him.

Barrabas climbed down from the driver's seat of the 4x4 and looked across the rolling foothills of the Wyoming Basin to the distant snow-covered Rockies, sniffing at the light breeze rolling past. It smelled clean and fresh, blowing down off the cold upper slopes of the mountains. Away from the cities, away from people—there still weren't many places in the world as empty as Wyoming was—his body seemed greedy for the invigorating purity.

After leaving the other mercs at the airport in Amarillo, Texas, Barrabas had flown straight to Cheyenne. There he'd picked up the rented Bronco four-wheel that brought him to the empty family ranch in Green River. Being back made him restless, but in a way he was glad. At least there were a few unspoiled places left where he could leave teeming humanity behind.

He walked toward the old house, the heels of his cowboy boots sinking into the soft black soil. His family had been dead and gone for more than a decade now, and the house was badly in need of painting and a new roof. It looked empty, unlived in, although beyond the lack of paint, Barrabas couldn't put his finger on the telltale signs that made it clearly so. It was something about sadness at the lack of life within its walls, Barrabas figured, as if a house could feel.

Billy Two had come here to find Barrabas once when Liam O'Toole was in trouble in Ireland, a prisoner sentenced to death by IRA execution squad. The crazy Indian's car had roared up the road in a cloud of billowing dust. He'd driven all the way from Arizona, and looked like a road zombie, his eyes refusing to blink. Somehow he had known Liam O'Toole was in trouble, although he couldn't explain how he knew. Barely ten minutes after he arrived the telephone rang and it was Jessup calling from New York. O'Toole had indeed been in trouble, and the SOBs were called in.

A figure now stood on the horizon, where a second ago Barrabas had seen only sky. The tiny black shape moved, shimmering slightly in the distance, and became distinguishable as it approached. It was a horse and his rider, slowly drawing closer and becoming larger.

Barrabas reminded himself that a Winchester rifle was on the rack in the Bronco, and his favored Browning inside his jacket.

Suddenly the horse bolted forward, the rider digging his legs against the animal's heaving sides to spur it on. Dust and clods of grass flew up underneath, and the horse's legs became a blur.

The Bronco was twenty-five feet away. Barrabas edged slightly toward it. A lasso uncoiled from the rider's upraised fist, the lariat twirling like the rotation of a planet in narrow ellipses. A long whooping yodel was amplified on a wave of wind, and carried clear across the fields.

A broad grin spread across Barrabas's face. He recognized that style: it was his old friend Jake Larraby. According to a local yarn the man had frozen two cattle rustlers dead in their tracks one time, coming across them at night and wailing out of the darkness like a coyote from hell.

Barrabas stood his ground and let the horseman come upon him. His horse was a brown beauty, with a white smudge down her snout, and her legs moved together like poetry. Jake's cowboy hat was clamped down over his eyes, and the tails of his long coat blew in the wind of his speed, while dust clouds rose behind him.

The lariat was suspended in a perfect circle, like a halo over his head, held in defiance of gravity by the fluid twirling of his arm. Jake worked the rope until it grew longer and the circle floated higher and farther out. With his other hand tight on the reins, he pulled, turning the horse to head straight at Barrabas. The tall white-haired warrior stared, faintly amused to be playing a familiar game after all these years.

Jake Larraby let out a shrill whoop and twisted the reins at the last moment. Clods of earth flew against Barrabas's leg as the horse veered to one side. The lariat floated down from the heavens, settling around Barrabas and spinning to the ground where it circled like a snake eating its tail.

Larraby ran the horse almost to the house before he reined her in, turned and trotted back to Barrabas, panting and laughing. He pulled her up next to the tall man.

"How's the last cowboy?" Barrabas shouted, waving and unable to resist a grin that spread from ear to ear.

"How's the unknown soldier?" Jake Larraby threw back the question without hesitation, grinning just as broadly.

They'd grown up together, many years ago, learned to shoot rifles, ride horses and make love with girls in the back seat of Jake's father's maroon Pontiac.

In the intervening years—too many of them—Barrabas's face had narrowed, and a few strong lines etched the dark weathered skin. Larraby had filled out, not with good times but with times well spent. The pinkish glow of broken veins just beneath the surface of the skin on Larraby's cheeks and nose bespoke a man who was a heavy drinker. Where gray crept up along Jake's sideburns to his temples, the colonel's hair was white liberally sprinkled with black, souvenir of a VC bullet he took in a certain battle on the Kap Long River.

Larraby swung off and slapped the horse's flank. She snorted and moved away, her sides heaving from the exertion of the run. He stepped forward, pulling up his hat to wipe his brow. Suddenly he froze midstep, his face twisted in pain. He drew his breath, his eyes went wide, and slowly his hand went to his lower back. He looked almost comical.

"Slipped a disk a few years back," he gritted between clenched jaws. Carefully he lowered one foot and maneuvered into position, twisted, and something snapped. He relaxed, and continued toward his old friend, smiling warmly.

Barrabas extended his hand.

"What is this?" Jake said in mock contempt. He pushed his old friend's hand away.

Laughing, the two men fell into each other's arms. Alternately they slapped each other on the back, and grabbed each other by the shoulders to shake hard.

"Last I saw you was out on Interstate 80 outside of Green River waiting for the Greyhound bus to Cheyenne and New York City. I guess you made it. I heard you were in the Army. You won that medal in Vietnam and never showed up to get it from the President."

Barrabas shrugged, but his eyes were still warm. "I guess everyone knows that story." It was an uncomfortable memory. "I'm not much of one for keeping in touch, Jake."

The cowboy started laughing. "If you could have found me, Nile. And even then..." For a moment Jake looked away. Quickly he turned back to Barrabas. "I moved around a lot, never more than a year or two in a lot of places—Montana, Nevada, couple years in Denver. I have a son in Santa Fe, and two daughters in Tucson." He laughed a little, almost in self-mockery. "The bottle got me for a while, too, Nile," he confessed.

"I'm sorry to hear that, Jake."

Jake put his hands up and quickly assured Barrabas in his gravelly voice. "Four years now, Nile. On the wagon."

Barrabas slapped his old friend on the back. "Congratulations." He motioned to the house. "Then I'll offer you coffee instead."

Once they were sitting around the table, they quickly realized that too many years had passed for them to bring each other up to date. They talked about pointless things for a while, the price of land, and people in Green River they both knew. Finally, when conversation lapsed, and an awkward silence fell upon them, Jake set down his coffee cup, stretched his feet and leaned his chair back on its rear legs.

"Why, Nile? How come you didn't turn up to collect that Medal of Honor? Folks back here were mighty proud of the native son, going to meet the President himself. Then you didn't show. Everyone around here, well, they felt let down, I think. And from what I heard about what you did, you sure did deserve the decoration you were getting."

Barrabas sighed inwardly. Many people had asked the same thing, and it did no good, really, to explain. It was something he'd done years ago. And there were too many good reasons for it. Because Jake was an old friend, he did his best to answer.

"I just couldn't take it when some of the real killers in Vietnam were still on the loose, some of them in government, working their way up the hierarchy in Washington."

Jake looked at Barrabas, surprised.

"It was drugs, you know," Barrabas continued. "By the end of the war, that's what Vietnam was. A major source of heroin exported from the poppy fields of Laos. American advisers and agents ran the cartel. The bastards. I don't know how many soldiers died because of it. Dozens? Hundreds? Thousands?"

"How'd..." Jake began.

"I stumbled onto it by accident. When I was colonel, some of my men disappeared into the jungle during the final onslaught that eventually brought the VC into Saigon. When I went after—well, they were dead by then. But I found out what was going on and who was behind it."

It was the best Nile Barrabas could do. Ultimately there were no words to explain that by the end of the war, he'd had enough—of Nam, and of all the politicians' lies heaped like shit on the dead bodies of fifty thousand young men. He had enough medals—a couple of Silver Stars, more than a few Purple Hearts. And he'd heard old generals make their speeches about brave young men who made the supreme sacrifice, giving their lives for freedom, and peace with honor. Those brave men had been his friends.

"And all that time, I saw myself and a hell of a lot of others tempered to hardness like steel in a forge," the mercenary said slowly. "We became men who suddenly had no choice about the killers we were, or how we had to live our lives. So I started a new policy. My own. Fighting was what I did best and I had enough anger to keep me going for fifty or a hundred wars. Kill or be killed. It was black and white, and it seemed like a good way to keep life simple."

"And now?" Jake's bushy gray eyebrows rose an inch.

"I'm not tired yet." Barrabas pushed his empty coffee cup away. His blue eyes clouded over, lost somewhere in thought. "And you?"

"Well, the Army wouldn't take me because of the old Larraby curse," Jake started slowly. He stared at the table, absentmindedly drawing circles on the wood with his index finger. He looked up at Barrabas.

"A little gurgle in the heart that the menfolk are born with. I took documented proof that both my daddy and granddaddy and a couple of uncles had it. The ones who weren't still alive had lived to ninety. But speaking of policy—they had one. So did the Navy. And the Air Force."

He sipped his coffee and continued. "A lot of ranches in Nevada needed young men badly, and they were only too happy to hire a young fellow on, long as they knew he wasn't a deserter. I worked as a cowhand for many a year and in many a place. Then I spent a few good years drinking enough liquor to learn that alcohol is my own personal devil. After I got on the wagon I got to be deputy in a little town in New Mexico—I'd been a deputy different times and situations before, but this time I decided to make a career of it. Moved up to Colorado and worked for the Boulder Police Department, and did a stint as a deputized state trooper in a little town near the Wyoming border."

"And now?"

Jake smiled. "Now I'm free-lance. I work for whatever rancher can pay my fee. You know I always had a bit of a reputation for tracking rustlers. Lot of people don't know we still have such a thing out here. But we do, and I'm the man who takes care of it. I'm the best. What about you, Nile?" Larraby teased. "You free-lance too?"

Barrabas broke into loud laughter. "You sure as hell can say that!"

Suddenly Larraby's eyes brightened with an idea. He took a gold pocket watch on a chain from inside his jacket and glanced at it. "Nile, I got to meet a client this afternoon and I want you to come."

"What's it all about, Jake?"

The old cowboy shook his head. "You won't believe it, Nile. Not unless you see it for yourself." He stood, and reached for his long canvas coat on a hook by the back door. "Four o'clock at that roadside diner on I-80 halfway to Little America. I'll see you there."

THE DINER HAD GROWN in the years Barrabas had been away, and since then the highway had been widened and connected to the interstate system that linked the entire country from coast to coast. Once it had been a small place, an aluminum-sided diner the size of a railway car, with a single long counter and an open kitchen.

When Barrabas turned the red 4x4 onto the access ramp, he could barely make out the original building behind a sea of parked semis, the gas station, service center, guest cabins and souvenir shop. The restaurant now had two sides—take out and eat in. The counter rippled like a snake to maximize the number of customers who could sit at it, and several rows of tables were placed between it and the plate-glass windows.

It was late afternoon, the sun low in the west, suspended just above the peaks of the Rockies. Already the snowcaps of Mount Isabel, Dead Knoll and Wyoming Peak were burnished with a rosy tinge from the slightest hint of sunset. In the valley, the air was hot and dry.

Barrabas sauntered into the restaurant, wallowing in cool conditioned air. A quick survey told him that Jake Larraby wasn't there yet. He sat at the counter and plucked a cardboard menu from the slot by the sugar and cream containers. A waitress in a trim white dress appeared on the other side of the counter.

"Coffee?" she asked, her voice mildly weary.

Barrabas nodded, looking up, and their eyes froze, caught by each other's. There was a moment of stunned silence. A grin spread slowly across Barrabas's face.

"Doris Amberton!"

And all the nights during his high school years flooded back to him. Nights spent in the back seat of a maroon Pontiac.

"Doris Larraby now," she told him. She was smiling, obviously glad to see him.

"You're married to Jake—"

"Married and divorced. So many years ago I don't even remember why we did it. I kept the name and the diamond. Found out the diamond was a zircon. And the Larraby name came with a reputation. Still, I kept it. Guess I needed a souvenir. You wanted coffee? I'll be right back."

He watched her walk down the counter, past the stainless steel racks of pies behind glass doors, the juicers, the toaster and the milk shakers. Under the waitress's dress she was trim, her curves still evident and—he couldn't help noticing—her breasts as ample as ever. She wore little makeup, and the years had marked her face with strength, not age. Her short curled hair was still jet-black, except for a shock of absolute white that rose from the left side of her forehead. Barrabas had to admit that in her own way, she was still a stunning beauty.

A warm smile played on Doris's face when she carried the steaming mug of coffee back to him.

"What brings you back to Green River, Nile?" she asked, slipping a pad from her apron pocket, writing out the check and flipping it facedown on the Arborite counter. "I never thought I'd see you around, after your folks died. And specially after—"

Barrabas raised his hands to stop her. "Don't tell me. The medal. People round here treat it like it was an obligation."

Doris nodded. "People round here got nothing better to do with their time than get upset about other people's business. I gave up on it years ago."

She leaned over the counter, the playful smile still tugging at her lips. Her scent was sweet and clean, and for Barrabas it brought back a rush of memories.

"Jake and I get along now that he's stopped drinking. But I'm my own girl, Nile, and what I do with my life is my own business. I have a mobile home out back of here. You ought to pay a visit. For old time's sake."

Nile reached across and laid his hand palm down over hers. There, the years of toil had left their mark, in calluses and distended veins. He squeezed, tempted by the offer, but resisting. He was rarely given to nostalgia because it was a way of being tied to the past.

"You've got a few scars over the years, too, haven't ya," Doris said, peering at his face from a few inches away.

Behind him, the door of the restaurant opened, and Barrabas felt the wave of hot outdoor air sweeping in. Doris's eyes moved that way.

"Speak of the devil." She straightened, turned around and grabbed another mug from the shelf behind her.

Jake Larraby shouted greetings across the restaurant to both of them, and strode over. He plunked himself down on the stool beside Barrabas just as Doris perfunctorily set down a second mug of hot coffee. When she turned, he reached across the counter and pinched her behind. Doris swung around and slapped his hand away, her brows rising to warn him. Her blue eyes, however, laughed.

"Jake, you just keep those paws off of me."

The cowboy turned to Barrabas. "She's still the best." He winked. "Doris, when we going to get married again, like Liz Taylor and all those other Hollywood stars you keep reading about in them supermarket checkout papers? It's proper if they do it."

"When hell freezes over, Jake. I can take care of myself, but I'll be damned if I'll start taking care of you. You boys like anything to eat?"

Barrabas looked to Jake. "What's the plan?"

"Rancher named Bob Cavendish, two miles up a side road from here. We should get there before dark. He's got something to show me."

The two men gulped their coffee and rose.

"You're still a looker, Doris," Barrabas told the waitress.

"Well, you watch out for this one." She pointed to Jake. "In case he tries to get you involved in his little business. The sheriff's still trying to find out how a couple of cattle rustlers got stranded in the badlands south of here a few weeks ago with a bullet hole in each head."

Jake shrugged as the two turned to leave. "It's the law of the west, Doris. Rustlers are scum and the fewer there are of them, the better off we all are. Me? I'm not saying nothing except that I just do my job."

"Now you come on back and see me while you're here, Nile," Doris told Barrabas. The mercenary turned and waved as the glass door closed behind him. Doris stood, arms akimbo, and watched until they drove away.

BOB CAVENDISH WAS an elderly man who lived with his wife on a ranch that extended to the shores of the Green River. They lived in a large log house, with bearskins hanging in the doorways, kerosene lights, an outhouse in the back and all the modern conveniences of television, dishwasher and microwave oven. It was an odd combination.

Cavendish was white-haired and stout, and his leathery skin testified to years spent outdoors in sun and rain and snow, and all manner of foul moods the weather had.

"What I got to show you is out on the range 'bout a mile from here," he told the two men. "We can take your 4x4 and do this real quick."

"We've had a rash of weird cattle killings," Jake explained to Barrabas for the first time. "Not just around here, either," he added mysteriously.

The ride across the fields behind the ranch house was bumpy, but the terrain presented no difficulty to the four-wheel drive. A quarter of a mile later, the land rolled down into a shallow valley, at the bottom of which an immense herd of shaggy brown cattle grazed.

Cavendish looked proudly at the fruits of his labor. "Took me forty years to build up that herd of cattle. I'll kill the bastard who's been doing this mutilation shit."

He spit a wad of chewing tobacco out the window, and the Bronco descended into the valley below.

The old rancher directed them to a spot several hundred yards from the flank of the immense herd, and the three men left the vehicle. The body of a cow lay on its side several dozen feet away. The men walked toward it.

Dusk had arrived early because the shadow of the mountains quickly spread across the valley. The heat from the day had dissipated very little, and warm winds danced across the rangelands. The sky turned purple in the west. In the distance, a thunderstorm could be seen, a great column of cumulonimbus cloud lit from within by jagged strokes of lightning. Thunder traveled across the valley, like the sound of approaching artillery.

Dehydration and insects devouring the flesh and organs had already reduced the cow to a mummy, little more than dried bones under the leathery brown hide. There was no smell, except the sweetness of grass carried on the warm moving air.

Despite the decay, the mutilation was clearly visible. The cow's udder had been removed with surgical precision. A gaping black slash where the blood had dried revealed that its throat had been cut. Barrabas stepped back and looked at the ground where the carcass lay, a stretch of grazed-over land.

There was no sign of bleeding. The ground around the dead cow was clean.

"Was it bled dry and dragged here from somewhere else?" Barrabas inquired, looking at Jake and Cavendish.

Larraby shook his head. "If we could find any sign of tire tracks that's what I'd say. But we never do. Just these things bled dry and mutilated like that."

"Happening up and down the Midwest," Bob Cavendish added, "every now and then, this place or that. Now they got one of mine. But what they do and why they do it, Lord have mercy on their souls." He shook his head gravely.

"Who is 'they'?" Barrabas demanded.

Cavendish and the old cowboy exchanged glances.

"Some say flying saucers, some say Satan worshipers," the old rancher said, spitting out another juicy wad of tobacco. "I even heard people say it's Jews!"

"While sometimes other people whisper it's an Aryan Nation trick," Jake Larraby said. He looked evenly at Barrabas.

Cavendish turned and walked a few steps away. He stood, a man of the land, ready for the constant struggle with nature. Behind him was the approaching storm. The column of cloud was stained red by the setting sun, and lit from within by lightning, like a city being bombed in the distance. Low in the eastern horizon under the storm, the light was purple. The wind rose, tugging at the men's Stetsons, bringing the smell of rain.

Cavendish abruptly turned back to face them. His face was red and he lashed out angrily. "You can whisper what you will! But don't talk about it!" he shouted. Thunder exploded behind him. "You don't dare talk about it!" His arms rose as he talked, then fell by his side abruptly. "Gonna rain. Let's go."

With that, he stalked off to the 4x4.

"He's a mighty scared man," Barrabas commented to Jake, staring after the retreating rancher.

"Aryan Nation, they're a pretty scary bunch," Jake said slowly. "You know about them?"

Barrabas nodded, disturbed by the irony of running into that bunch for the second time that day. "Just the basics. I didn't know they were around these parts."

"They're everywhere, along with their friends called the Posse Comitatus. They call it the second American revolution. They believe money should be abolished and only gold and silver used. They think the sixteenth amendment, which allows the government to have a banking system, is illegal. The only power they recognize is the sheriff of the county. And they own some of them, too. And they raise their kids, have them born at home, keep them out of school, so no one knows they even exist. Call them sovereigns. They say the government in Washington is illegal and call it ZOG—for Zionist Occupation Government. And they're armed to the teeth."

"What exactly do they want?" Barrabas asked. "Other than to get their buddies out of prison in New Mexico."

Larraby looked closely at Barrabas, his eyes narrowed. "You know something about this after all, don't you, Nile, more than just the basics."

"A little," Barrabas admitted.

"Well, all they want is an independent state in the Pacific Northwest. Oregon and Washington are to be Posse country, you know, racially pure," he said, with contempt for the last two words. "How long you gonna be around, Nile?"

"A few days. What's up?"

"About time you and I had a little adventure." Jake slapped at Barrabas's chest, and pointed to the mutilated and mummified cow lying at their feet. He had a know-it-all expression, and in his eyes was a look that spelled trouble. He started walking toward the Bronco. "I'll have to get something going and let you know," he promised with a laugh.

**4**

The big Mack truck picked up speed as it went down the grade in low gear because of its heavy load. The two-lane Idaho highway coiled around the side of the mountain. On the other side, a vertical drop went down two hundred feet. There was a spectacular view to the south of the Great Salt Lake Desert. As far as the eye could see, the land was barren rock, and in the distance salt flats shimmered in the hot noonday sun.

The truck, despite its size, easily caught up to a two-door gray Cadillac with Montana plates traveling the double nickel speed limit to the max. The large car rode low on the highway, weighted down with luggage and four passengers. Joe and Hilda Evans were returning their niece and nephew to do summer work at the university after having a two-week summer break at their ranch. Paul and Jennifer were the best examples of responsible young people who also knew how to have fun.

The truck driver honked once, shifted gear and pulled out. Quickly, the truck gathered speed, passing the slow Caddy and pulling back into the right lane, where it gained distance on the slow-moving luxury car.

Paul had been sitting back, relaxing in the rear seat, but now he leaned forward to speak to his aunt and uncle. "Look at that sign—Danger—Radioactive Material. It's not often anybody sees things like that. Makes you kind of shiver."

His uncle glanced at the speedometer to ensure the needle pointed precisely to fifty-five miles an hour. "It's probably just a load of burned-out fuel from one of the nuclear power plants. Most likely going to a nuclear waste dump they put out in the desert somewhere."

"If you ask me, he's traveling pretty fast for someone with a hazardous load," Hilda Evans harrumphed, looking up momentarily from her knitting and peering over the top of her reading glasses.

"I need to freshen up at a rest room pretty soon," Jennifer said, putting her hand up to her rich flow of auburn hair.

Hilda glanced at her watch. "My lordy, Joe. It's almost one o'clock already and we haven't stopped for lunch yet."

"Well, there's not many places to stop out here," Joe snapped.

"You're right, I'm starving," Jennifer admitted. "But I'd rather have your good cooking, Aunt Hilda."

"I believe there's a highway rest stop a few miles after the tunnel," Joe told Hilda.

Jennifer's aunt turned around to look at the two handsome young people in the back seat. "Well, I'm glad you liked my cooking. You both look healthy enough. It was fun having you stay with us! Made me feel young again."

They exchanged smiles, then returned their attention to the scenery. The highway leveled at the bottom of a mountain valley, with sheer rock walls rising sixty to eighty feet on either side of the road.

The truck slowed as it lost the momentum of the descent from the hill, and in a few minutes the Cadillac was behind it again. Another car pulled up behind the Caddy, and soon the truck was leading a long line of vehicles that snaked along the mountain highway. A mile ahead, the Webber Tunnel, half a mile of roadway blasted through the middle of a mountain, was a tiny black hole.

In the cab of the big truck, Tony Paccatello nudged his partner, Nick Soames, who was snoozing in the passenger seat.

"Hey buddy, there's the tunnel. You take over in five miles after we hit the diner, and I'll grab me some shut-eye."

Nick started and opened his eyes. "We there already?"

"Five more miles after the tunnel," Tony told him. The burly truck driver swore. "Goddamn if there ain't construction up ahead." He checked the rearview mirror before slowing and silently cursed the driver of the Cadillac, who was now tailgating him.

A quarter mile in front of the tunnel, a battered pickup truck with county markings blocked one lane of the highway. The work crew, wearing fluorescent orange safety vests, were setting up orange cones to reroute traffic to one side, and a young man with shoulder-length blond hair held a Caution sign. Tony Paccatello hit the brakes and shifted down, slowing the truck. The Cadillac came dangerously close to the rear mudguards, then braked as well.

The young man holding the Caution sign waved the truck through. Paccatello hit the gas and shifted up. The diesel engine roared and the Mack truck gained speed, heading toward the gaping tunnel entrance fifty feet ahead.

As soon as the truck passed him, the young man spun the amber Caution sign around. The other side was red and said Stop.

"Quickly, dear!" Hilda Evans said sharply to her husband in the Cadillac. "Get in behind the truck or we'll have to wait here for half an hour waiting for traffic to come through the tunnel from the other side.''

Joe Evans hit the gas too abruptly, and the car jerked forward, throwing his wife and the two people back in their seats.

"Hey! Hey you! Stop!" the blond man with the traffic sign cried, waving his arms and the Stop sign, and trying to run in front of the car.

Joe Evans calmly stayed on course, steering the Cadillac slightly to one side to avoid the construction worker. Two other construction workers began waving at the Cadillac and running toward it. Evans kept his foot on the accelerator, until he closed to within several feet of the rear of the truck. Both vehicles gained speed and disappeared into the yawning black hole bored through the mountain.

On the highway, the construction workers threw their arms into the air and looked at one another, exasperated.

Then the blond man started laughing. "It's their asses." Sonny Doule shrugged. "If they wanna be in such a hurry."

He unclipped a walkie-talkie from his belt, pulled out the antenna and aimed it at the tunnel. Raising the microphone to his lips, he spoke quickly. "Blue team One, this is Two. A second vehicle has entered the tunnel. We'll take care of them, too." He pushed the antenna back down and clipped the radio to his belt, smiling at the other two workers. "More crispy critters!" He laughed again.

The other two workers, both men in their thirties, looked at him. "You've got no heart, Sonny, no heart whatsoever."

Sonny didn't look as though he cared. He faced the oncoming traffic, holding the Stop sign in front of him. Traffic slowed and came to a halt, with anxious travelers sticking their heads out their windows to see what was going on.

Quickly, the workers placed the rest of the orange cones along the road, blocking it completely. They dragged a large sign reading Blasting Ahead, Temporary Delay, to the center of the highway. Then they jumped into the pickup truck. Sonny was at the wheel. The pickup sped into the tunnel after the Mack truck and the Cadillac, leaving a dozen mystified and fuming drivers lined up at the barricade behind them.

In the tunnel, the headlights of the Mack truck slithered along blasted walls of solid rock, cutting a swath through air as black as ink. The tunnel curved very slightly to the right along its half-mile course. The headlights of the Cadillac reflected from Paccatello's side mirror into his eyes until he reached outside and twisted it, turning the reflection elsewhere. In the Caddy, Evans was oblivious to the fact that his brights were on.

"There's that construction," Nick said. Ahead in the darkness, a red light flashed on and off. The headlights of the truck picked up reflectors on parked vehicles. Men moved in front of the lights, waving the truck to a halt.

Joe shifted down and braked to within a few feet of the men. He stuck his head out the window. Two men scrambled into a wrecker in the opposite lane.

Construction workers with beards and wearing dark overalls fanned around the cab. The wrecker roared to life, its headlights came on, and it took off down the tunnel.

"Now what on earth..." Hilda Evans said in an exasperated voice when the Mack truck's brake lights went on and it slowed to a halt in front of them.

Still oblivious to his tailgating, Joe Evans stopped a foot away. His brights turned the polished aluminum trailer into an enormous reflective light, illuminating the tunnel. Almost immediately, the blinding white headlights of the wrecker swept up beside the truck, while the pickup truck from outside closed in behind. The Evanses put their hands to their eyes. Men jumped from both trucks and closed in on the Cadillac, their faces grim.

"Those men have rifles!" Paul said in an awed tone that was edged with incredulous fear.

"Now, Paul!" his aunt admonished, turning to the back seat. "That's no kind of joke to make—"

Joe Evans found words forming in his throat, but his tongue was paralyzed and he was unable to speak.

Sonny drew near the car. He raised his gun and the window in the door exploded. Bullets thunked into Evans's head and threw him across the seat, covering his wife with blood.

Hilda screamed, beating her arms hysterically in front of her to fend off the sudden nightmare. A single shot from Sonny's gun silenced her forever. Instinctively the two in the back slipped to the floor and huddled together for protection.

In vain.

Sonny opened the back door, grabbed Paul's elbow and dragged him from the car. Paul struggled, though he felt hopeless when he saw the man's cool efficiency. Sonny aimed, and Paul's eyes widened in panic. Sonny pulled the trigger, and the back of Paul's skull blew off.

Jennifer screamed hysterically, pushing against the door from the floor of the car and kicking at the blond man.

He leaned forward, pointing his gun at her, with his arm straight. "You should be thankful," he said.

He shot her twice. The first one, to the heart, killed her. The second one was for good measure, he told himself as he let her go.

He waved to the other men climbing from the wrecker. One immediately began to tamp plastic explosives around the iron bolts that locked the rear door of the trailer.

At the head of the doomed cavalcade, Tony's door was yanked open and the truck driver stared straight into the eye of an Uzi. The Israeli submachine gun spit, and bloody holes zipped up his body from crotch to forehead. He jiggled wildly, the bullets throwing him to the ceiling of the cab. Then he fell, tumbling to the road like a straw man.

Nick left his seat with a crowbar in hand. He kicked the door open, catching Sonny's man off guard. The crowbar came down, sinking deep into the attacker's skull, disappearing in a spurt of blood. Then the trucker felt deep terrible pain in his legs and heard gunfire. The world went silent. His legs collapsed beneath him and a fire burned upward, flaring into excruciating agony. When he looked, his knees had turned to blood and shattered bone.

A man stood over him, and poked his face with the muzzle of his gun. The barrel was hot.

"You're gonna pay for that," the man said. He pointed to the dead buddy with a crowbar embedded sideways in his head, and stepped back. He shouted to the other men swarming around the truck. "Gimme one of those," he demanded, motioning with his arm. "I want to keep this one alive."

Nick propped himself on his elbows and tried to drag himself backward. The pain almost snuffed out his consciousness, yet through the haze, his nostrils caught the familiar smell. Gasoline. The attacker stood over him, pouring gas from a two-gallon can. The noxious liquid splashed into his face, over his clothes, and collected in puddles on the road. The man moved away to join others around the truck. The plastics had been placed and wired, and Sonny and his men took cover on one side of the truck. The explosion echoed dully up and down the length of the tunnel. The locks on the trailer snapped in a burst of sparks and molten metal, and the steel doors hung crazily on their hinges.

The men swarmed inside. One man backed up the wrecker until it was within a few feet of the open doors. Several men heaved metal ramps from the back of the wrecker to bridge the space between the two vehicles. The hydraulic winch was lowered, its cable and iron hook pulled inside the truck trailer.

"This one." Sonny directed his men. The trailer was filled with metal drums painted bright yellow, wedged securely in wooden frames. Quickly, the cable and hook were wrapped around the one closest to the door.

"Go!" someone shouted. In the cab of the wrecker, the driver started the winch. The hydraulics picked up slack on the cable, groaned, and slowly the crate and drum tipped.

"Fucking heavy," someone commented. Three men jumped behind it as it fell over. The cable was readjusted and quickly the drum was pulled across the metal bridge into the back of the wrecker.

Sonny called to one of the men. "Fix the Cadillac," he ordered, handing him a length of rubber tubing. The man nodded with a smile. He went to the luxury car, inserted one end of the tube into the gas tank, and sucked on the other end, which he then held low to the ground. He spit out a mouthful of gas. The clear amber liquid gushed through the tube onto the road.

The men climbed aboard the pickup and the wrecker. The two vehicles sped past the semi truck, the wrecker gathering speed and heading for the end of the tunnel. The pickup truck slowed by the cab of the big semi. Headlights picked out the truck driver, still alive and lying half upright in a pool of blood, his knee-capped legs useless in front of him. Nick Soames lifted a hand to his pain-crazed eyes to shield them from the bright headlights.

Sonny glanced at his watch. They had accomplished everything in four and a half minutes—thirty seconds less than planned.

"Let's get out of here!" Sonny yelled. The last two men jumped into the back of the pickup truck. The driver hit the gas, and the pickup lurched forward, jolting over Soames's legs. The wounded man screamed. The truck roared down the tunnel, then screeched to halt 250 feet away.

The tunnel, lit by headlights from the semi and the pickup, was almost quiet except for the idling of engines. Sonny reached for an M-16 on the rifle rack behind him. An incendiary grenade was attached to the adapter on the end of the barrel. He twisted around and leaned out the window, firing toward the lights of the Mack truck.

The driver hit the gas and the pickup raced forward. Sonny pulled himself in. Behind them the tunnel was lit by a brilliant white flash. A wall of flame enveloped the truck, racing greedily through the pools of gasoline.

Nick Soames screamed once before he was devoured by thermite fire burning at more than one thousand degrees above zero. Leaping across the puddles of gasoline, a sheet of bright yellow flame consumed the Mack truck and the Cadillac, reducing the corpses to charred bone.

The concussion wave rolled down the highway, pushing against the speeding getaway truck. Sonny leaned back in the seat, rolling up the window. He had a big smile on his face.

They had the plutonium and they were right on time.

"Next stop Arkansas," Doule, Jr., hooted and slapped the driver on the shoulder. "Ain't nothing going to stop the second American revolution now."

A DAY AFTER ARRIVING in Green River, Barrabas decided to sell out, and drove into Rock Springs to see a realtor. On the radio on the way in he heard a news bulletin about a disaster that had taken place a few hours earlier at the Webber Tunnel in Idaho. A construction accident had somehow caused a fire that led to gas tanks exploding and the deaths of an as yet undetermined number of people.

Barrabas changed the station, searching in vain up and down the dial for some soothing classical music, or soft pop. He wasn't working, and preferred to leave the world and its problems behind.

Rock Springs was a big town for Wyoming—more than twenty thousand people lived there. The cars were parked diagonally up and down the long wide main street, which was fronted by stores, barbershops, doctors' offices and a few bars.

Barrabas pulled the red Bronco into a space several doors down from a 7-Eleven convenience store, and left it, not bothering to lock the doors. At the real estate office across the street, a realtor named Casey Wiggins was expecting him. She was a plump matronly woman in her late thirties, with short red hair and a helpful manner.

After explaining the state of the local market to Barrabas, the woman concluded, "And I'm afraid what with farm prices generally these days, Mr. Barrabas, I don't think we could get much more than—"

"Money doesn't matter," Barrabas interrupted. His lawyer in Geneva assured him he was a millionaire several times over, if he ever bothered to count. "It's a matter of letting go. I've thought about it a long time. I'll never be here again."

"And where do you live now?"

Barrabas laughed lightly. He'd forgotten about that. Most people had addresses. "A hotel room, somewhere." He had lived that way for almost twenty years now.

"You're in business, Mr. Barrabas?"

"Private enterprise." He laughed again, this time standing to go.

Outside the air was stifling and dry, the rays of the sun relentless. The noonday light was almost white. Rock Springs had the one-story, flat-roofed look of a cowboy town. Except for the cars and pickups parked side by side up and down Main Street, it could have been the wild West. Few people strolled the sidewalks in the hot afternoon, preferring the air-conditioned comfort of home or office.

There was nothing much more for Barrabas to do except pick up a few things from the old house and drive to Cheyenne where he could get a plane to New York. Then Europe or somewhere else—at least until the next phone call from Walker Jessup made it specific.

He headed for the 7-Eleven convenience store where his jeep was parked.

FIVE HOURS AFTER the bloody hijacking in the Webber Tunnel, Chuka Wrathe steered a battered blue van onto the exit ramp leading from Interstate 80 to the business district of the small Wyoming town of Rock Springs. Sonny sat in the passenger seat beside him. Spiker and Wilco were in back with the goods from the Mack truck.

The stolen casket of radioactive material had been transferred from the wrecker to the back of the old van at a rendezvous site in the low rolling hills of eastern Idaho. An hour later, traveling by secondary highways, the men crossed the border into Wyoming and met Interstate 80.

The heavy casket of plutonium in the back of the van held down their speed. They were forced to stop constantly for gasoline, each time braced for the appearance of a state trooper or police car. And sometimes, working their way up a long steep grade on the mountainous route, they found themselves reduced almost to a crawl. There would be no easy getaway if someone came after them.

The radio continued to broadcast news of the Webber Tunnel disaster, but so far it was still attributed to an accident involving a construction crew. Sooner or later, however, investigators were going to find the brass casings of bullets among the charred remains of human bodies, someone would realize the truck involved had been carrying reprocessed, weapons-grade plutonium to a storage site in Utah.

But until then, there was no possibility of roadblocks. So far everything had gone without a hitch.

Chuka pulled into a parking spot in front of the 7-Eleven in downtown Rock Springs. Sonny, Spiker and Wilco went in for supplies—cigarettes, potato chips and coffee.

BILL STEAD HAD BEEN on the go with his roving cameraman since 9:00 a.m. the day before. That made it thirty-six hours without sleep.

The celebrated anchorman had built his career on a solid reputation for single-handed investigative reports on controversial subjects. When the nuclear scientist had been kidnapped a week earlier in Los Alamos, by coincidence Stead had already been working on an in-depth newscast on the Aryan Nation.

After the discovery of the massacre in Amarillo, Texas, his telephone calls to a few people who owed him favors got him to the scene within hours. When he and his cameraman were escorted off the premises by FBI agents, he had contacted his inside source again.

Within an hour the man had faxed him the latest items from the FBI files. One was a series of computer-enhanced stills from the hidden video camera that had filmed the Los Alamos kidnapping. The faces of several of the kidnappers were clearly recognizable—and unidentified.

One in particular struck him. It was a young blond man, who looked wholesome enough to be a California surfer. The photograph showed him with a gun pressed into the neck of a guard who knelt in submission in front of him.

The second item that was leaked to Stead was a list of known Aryan Nation compounds and safehouses through the Midwest.

By early afternoon, Stead and his cameraman had arrived in Cheyenne, picked up a network car and headed west on the interstate. Bill Stead figured that if he couldn't get information from the FBI types like Claymore Jeffries, he might as well go straight to the horse's mouth. He'd see what the leaders of the Aryan Nation had to say for themselves.

It might win him another award. Or if there was a book, even a Pulitzer. It didn't occur to him that it might be dangerous.

Their first destination had been a farm outside of Rawlins, a town just off the interstate. To their great disappointment, the place was empty. Crusted-over dishes and dirt inside the house indicated that no one had been there in some time. Stead and his cameraman got back into the white network station wagon and returned to the interstate. Their next target was a place in Utah.

The day was hot, and on the highway it got hotter. The station wagon had no air-conditioning. Neither man had slept in two days, and the highway sign pointing to Rock Springs came as a relief.

"Let's find a hotel where we can lay up for the night," Stead said.

His cameraman was only too happy to oblige. He turned the steering wheel to the right, and the car swung across the lanes onto the exit ramp.

Meanwhile, Chuka waited patiently for Sonny and the others to finish inside the 7-Eleven, and scarcely noticed the white station wagon with the logo of a major television network stenciled on the door panel that pulled into the parking lot beside him.

He cast it a nonchalant glance. A short trim man wearing a blue windbreaker got out on the far side. Chuka thought he looked familiar. An older man, practically bald, climbed out of the driver's seat.

The two men moved toward the rear door of the station wagon. Then Chuka saw the network decal on the door panel, and it hit him like a sudden blow to the solar plexus. A television newsman.

He had just started to wonder if he should warn Sonny, when the blond young killer walked out of the convenience store with Wilco and Spiker behind him.

Bill Stead saw them and gasped. They were the faces from the computer-enhanced stills he'd received a few hours earlier.

First it occurred to him that this was the scoop of his lifetime. His second thought was to call the state troopers. But by then the men would be long gone. And so would be the possibility of an exclusive scoop.

A seasoned media reporter, Bill Stead acted on his first idea, not his second. He turned to the cameraman, who was reaching in through the open back window of the station wagon for a suitcase.

"Get out the camera and start filming!" Stead muttered carefully from the side of his mouth.

"But—"

"Now!" Stead snapped. He swung his tape recorder out the window of the car and strode forward, presenting himself to Sonny Doule.

"Excuse me, I'd like to talk to you about that kidnapping in Los Alamos. Bill Stead, *Report on Facts*—" He thrust the microphone into Sonny's face.

The young sovereign drew back, then with a sneer pushed past, knocking Bill Stead out of the way. The cameraman hoisted the video camera to his shoulder and turned it on Stead and Doule. Its motor whirred and the tape rolled.

"What the fuck you think you're—" Sonny swung around and reached for the camera. The cameraman stepped back, keeping it focused on him. Bill Stead moved between the two men, thrusting the microphone repeatedly at Sonny's face, and shooting rapid-fire questions at him.

Sonny backed away, for a moment nonplussed at being videotaped.

"Get them!" he shouted to the others.

Chuka jumped from the truck and grabbed for the camera, his fist closing around the protruding lens. He tugged, trying to rip it from the cameraman's hands. The cameraman shouted, keeping his hands gripped tightly around the end of the camera. Chuka booted him in the stomach. The kick threw the older man back against the plate-glass window of the convenience store. He doubled up around his precious camera in a last-ditch effort to protect it.

Moving calmly, Spiker and Wilco reached into the back of the van and drew out gleaming chrome bicycle chains.

Bill Stead raced to his cameraman's side. The man was groaning with pain. Obviously, the situation was getting out of hand.

He retreated, pulling the cameraman with him, while Sonny and Chuka fanned around them. Spiker and Wilco approached from the van, their chains swinging menacingly.

Stead slammed against something hard. It was the wall of the building facing the parking lot.

The four men closed in.

At that moment, across the street, Nile Barrabas left Wiggins Realty and walked to his parked Bronco. He noticed the commotion in the parking lot of the convenience store, where a pack of hostile young men surrounded two others, who cowered against a brick wall.

Barrabas raced across the parking lot. "You guys got a problem?" he demanded.

Sonny swung around and looked at the tall, white-haired man who faced him. He didn't like people spoiling his game. Chuka and the others turned, too.

Wilco and Spiker gripped one end of the chains and let them swing slowly at their sides.

"Lookie-lookie, we got a do-gooder wants to stick his nose in our business," Sonny sneered. He stepped forward, his teeth clenched with cruel anger. He went for the tall man.

Barrabas slammed his fist into Sonny's mouth. He felt the flesh crush and tear against teeth, the teeth snapping, the sudden warmth of blood. Doule stopped short, almost as if he was trying to decide what to do. Then the force of the blow tossed him backward and slapped him to the sidewalk.

Spiker and Wilco joined the assault.

Barrabas ducked, feeling a chain slice through the air inches above his head. It was the man with the shaved head and funny pants.

Wilco moved on the razor's edge of adrenaline, propelled on a single course, to destroy the man who wanted to interfere. But it was all happening so fast. Before he could pull his chain back, Barrabas darted in and grabbed the arm that held the weapon, his fingers tightening around Wilco's wrist like a steel manacle. Quickly, he worked with the man's momentum and used its force to twist and flatten the elbow against his shoulder.

Roger Wilco's feet left the ground, but Barrabas didn't flip him. He jerked hard until he heard the elbow joint shatter. Wilco's anguished scream was deafening. Barrabas dropped him in time to see the second chain whiz through space.

Spiker attacked. Again Barrabas retreated just as the chain zipped by. This time he came back with a double forearm lock. In one fluid motion, he pivoted around Chandler's arm, pulling it over his shoulder. He kept twisting until he was sideways against the attacker. Then he kneed the punk hard in the stomach.

Spiker's eyes widened in the shock of excruciating pain. He gurgled and curled over, clutching his solar plexus, lungs empty, diaphragm paralyzed. Barrabas swung away from him, simultaneously chopping the back of his neck with his powerful forearm. Spiker crumpled into a twisted ball, writhing in agony.

Against the wall of the convenience store, Bill Stead struggled valiantly with Chuka. The diminutive reporter had thrown himself onto the bigger man's back. He gripped his arms around Chuka's neck while trying to kick him in the kidneys. Chuka finally threw him off and came for Barrabas, his nostrils flared and face reddened by fury.

Not far away, the cameraman darted back and forth, from brawl to brawl. He was videotaping everything.

Chuka grabbed Spiker's chain from the pavement where the incapacitated punk had dropped it. He swung at Barrabas.

When the chain slashed through the air at him, Barrabas leaped at it instead of swerving to avoid it.

Surprised by the unexpected move, Chuka jumped backward. When he pulled the chain away, it went slack. Barrabas's long arms went out, and he clamped his hands around his attacker's wrist. He started crushing. The punk's mouth opened wide in a big silent scream, and his fingers spread apart. The chain dropped.

Barrabas grabbed it before it fell and let go of the wrist. He swung, snagging Chuka around the neck with the chain. Chuka clawed desperately at his throat, coughing for air and trying to get the cold steel off him. Quickly Barrabas pulled the man forward and down, bringing his knee up, and bashing him in the forehead with a loud hollow knock.

Chuka staggered backward, and fell against the plate-glass window, his dazed head lolling loosely on his shoulders. The other men scrambled to their feet, their faces registering shock, disbelief and fear. Sonny was already at the wheel of the blue van.

He veered in an arc around the white station wagon while Spiker, Chuka and the injured Wilco fled for the open side door. Sonny hit the accelerator. The tires spun, throwing up clouds of smoke and the smell of burned rubber. The wheels screeched as they regained traction and the blue van shot off the curb into the traffic on Main Street.

Barrabas made no effort to give chase. He slapped his hands across the legs of his pants to brush them off.

Bill Stead slowly pulled himself up from the ground, brushing the dust from his coat. He approached Barrabas.

"Bill Stead, *Report on Facts*." He smiled, extending his hand.

The arm of the cameraman crossed between the two men. He handed the reporter a videotape. "Six o'clock news," he said proudly. "I got the whole fight."

"All of it?" Stead said with amazement, reaching for the cassette. Barrabas's arm swooped out and plucked the cassette from the cameraman's hand first.

Surprised, the two television men instinctively reacted by diving for it, but Barrabas held it high over their heads and stepped back. "No deal. I'm not going on TV," he told them smiling, almost bemused.

Stead looked briefly horrified but regained his composure. He swallowed and smiled benignly. "But you don't understand. I'm Bill Stead, anchorman for a national news program on a public television network. *The* Bill Stead. Surely you've heard of me?"

He reached inside his jacket pocket and snapped a business card at Barrabas. Flashing a smile with too many perfect teeth, he extended his hand. "I thank you for what you did, sir. You're a genuine knight in shining armor."

Tentatively, Barrabas shook the proffered hand. "I'll tell you what I'll do," he told Stead, waving the video-cassette in front of him. "I'll keep your card and I'll return this to you after I have the parts that show me deleted. You can use the rest. Take it or leave it, but you won't get it back before then."

Stead swallowed nervously and put his hands on his hips. He peered both ways, up and down the street, then looked at Barrabas again, making an attempt at a friendly laugh.

"Now why don't we find somewhere we can have a drink and talk it over," he offered, slapping Barrabas's shoulder, one good ol' boy to another.

"There's nothing to talk about. I don't go on TV, that's all." Firmly clutching the cassette, Barrabas started to walk away.

"No! Wait," Stead pleaded, running after him. He held his hands out, beseeching Barrabas to hand back the tape.

"Those men may have been involved in a criminal activity," Stead pleaded.

"You mean you knew those men were wanted by the police, and you just started filming them?" Barrabas remonstrated. "They could have killed you!"

Stead shrugged carelessly. "But it's also exactly the kind of material that makes my TV show a hit! And besides, we survived. It didn't happen."

Barrabas shook his head in disbelief. Bill Stead was definitely a type, the kind who went out on a limb while expecting someone else to be there with a butterfly net to catch him.

"I have your card," Barrabas reiterated, holding up the tape. He backed away.

"Boss, you're not going to give in to this guy!" the cameraman rushed forward and demanded fearfully. "He'll never send it back. He'll sell it to another network. Give me that, you—" He threw himself at Barrabas.

Stead stepped in front of him, and held the man back. "This guy saved our necks a few minutes ago." Stead turned back to Barrabas. "Promise?" he asked skeptically.

"Promise," the mercenary nodded. "You'll be surprised." Barrabas turned toward the Bronco, slipping Stead's card into his pocket and gripping the cassette.

**5**

"I want that fucker dead!" Sonny screamed from the driver's seat of the battered blue van. "That white-haired fucker, he dies!"

He shook his fist, tightly wrapped by a blood-soaked bandanna, then he winced, and pressed it against his mouth again. His lips were broken and swollen where Barrabas's fist had struck, and there was a bloody hole in place of the right upper incisor that had been there a few minutes earlier.

With his other arm he swung the steering wheel hard. Tires squealed, and the van leaned sharply to the left as he negotiated the curving ramp onto Interstate 80.

In the back Roger Wilco screamed with pain. He leaned against a frame of the heavy casket in the middle, his face blanched from the excruciating agony. With the other hand he clutched his broken arm. It swayed uselessly at his side with every movement of the vehicle.

Spiker sat across from the injured man. He leaned forward between the seats to shout to Sonny and Chuka. "You gotta slow down! Every time this thing jolts he's in pain."

"I can't help it," Sonny shouted back. "It's the weight from that fucking crate that's causing us to bounce around! The mother must weigh half a ton. You can feel it dragging on the engine when you try to accelerate."

He veered right and braked where the ramp turned into a merge lane, pulling over to the shoulder.

"Here! You drive!"

Angrily Sonny jumped from the cab and stalked around to the other side. Chuka climbed over the gearbox and settled at the wheel. When Sonny was back in the van, he hit the gas.

"Some fucking vehicle to split fast in," Sonny muttered darkly, still dabbing the cloth at his lacerated lips.

Chuka grabbed the wheel and laboriously wound it to the left to bring the van in line with the road. The vehicle gained momentum on the shoulder and merged into the first lane behind a big semi truck that flew past.

"Those chains were Wilco's idea, man," Chuka snarled when he had control. "If he'd carried his MAC-10 like I told him to, that wouldn't have happened."

"Yeah, and we'd already have half the state troopers in Wyoming on our tail," Spiker called from the back. Wilco was squirming with pain and whimpering. "And if they found out what we had in this crate here and where we were going with it..."

"Not if we had the MAC-10s," Chuka shot back. "Then we'd have half the state troopers in Wyoming dead." He laughed.

They passed a highway sign indicating a secondary road crossing.

Spiker leaned into the front seat again. "Look, Wilco's hurting pretty bad. We gotta get him to a doctor and get that arm taken care of."

Sonny nudged Chuka on the shoulder to get his attention.

"Take this exit off the interstate," he ordered, pointing out the window. Chuka obliged him, easing the loaded van onto the off ramp.

"Where we going?" Spiker demanded.

"Back to Rock Springs, Wyoming. I got some business to take care of." He looked calmly across the seat at the driver. "You too, right, Chuka?"

"Right, Sonny. Dead right."

"If we go for a doctor there, they'll be looking for us—" Spiker started.

"Man, you are a dumb one." Sonny shook his head slowly. He turned back to Chuka and nodded. The driver calmly pulled the van onto the road and crossed to the ramp leading onto the interstate in the opposite direction.

"We really going back there?" Spiker cried in disbelief. "We gotta get this thing to Arkansas by tomorrow." He jerked his thumb at the wooden crate.

"So what are they going to do if we're a day late? Fire us?" Sonny demanded. "Chuka, keep driving."

"What in hell for?" Spiker demanded.

Sonny clenched the bloody handkerchief in his fist and shook it in front of Spiker's nose. "We got unfinished business with that white-haired guy and that reporter asshole."

"And what are we supposed to do with Wilco's broken arm?"

Sonny turned back to the driver. "Chuka Chuka Chuka," he said as if he were calling for a dog. "Let's stop at the next rest area."

Chuka looked sideways and saw in Sonny's eyes what he was thinking. He slowly returned the smile and gave a little nod.

Ten minutes later, he pulled the van off the highway at a spot where picnic tables and a rest room waited for the convenience of tourists. There was a young forest of short thin pines behind the area, running for several miles up the interstate.

A red Pontiac with four elderly passengers inside and suitcases on the roof rack lumbered slowly out of the rest area as the van drove in. Otherwise it was deserted. Chuka braked in front of the rest rooms.

"I'll take care of it," Sonny muttered, hopping out. He ran around the back, pulled open the door and reached for Roger Wilco, grabbing his arm. It was the broken one. Wilco screamed with anguish.

"What are...wh-wh—what are you..." Wilco sobbed.

Sonny hauled him from the van. He planted his boot on Wilco's buttocks and propelled him roughly toward the edge of the forest.

Wilco stumbled forward and fell. Sonny was on top of him, hauling him to his feet and pushing him forward again. Wilco screamed and begged him to stop. His broken arm hung uselessly at his side.

In the van, Spiker was about to leap from the back when Chuka suddenly stood in the way, his arms folded across his chest and a defiant grin on his face. Sonny pushed and shoved Wilco into the forest.

It was hot in the woods, the rays of the sun beating down through tiers of branches, and dappling the forest ground with dancing spots of yellow. Sonny had a German Luger stuffed carelessly in the side pocket of his black leather jacket, the safety not even on, a gift from his father when he turned thirteen.

The blond punk pulled it out and pressed the barrel into the back of Wilco's head, just above his neck.

Holding him by the collar of his black leather jacket, Sonny fired.

Wilco's forehead blew open, a big piece of the skull flying against the tree trunk, chunks of glistening brain tissue splattering everywhere. The body flopped forward and shivered with final nerve spasms. The head lay sideways, the upper portion exposing the scant remains of Wilco's brain in his broken skull. Considering the nature of the savage death, the open eyes were dull and surprisingly peaceful.

Sonny plunged the Luger into his pocket and walked back to the parking lot. The other two were waiting uncomfortably, embarrassed by the lethality of Sonny's violent tantrums. There was no need to ask where Wilco was. They had heard the shot.

"We gotta go back. That cameraman got the whole fucking fight down. We gotta get it back," Doule told Spiker and Chuka in a calm quiet voice.

He faced them, arms akimbo, his tongue worrying the bloody gap where until recently there had been a front incisor.

"I saw the white-haired guy come out of a place across the street from the store just before it happened. We find the reporter and get the videotape. We find the other guy, we kill him."

In Washington, D.C. the cocktail party was already in high gear when Walker Jessup lumbered through the front door. He handed his hat to the butler and mopped his forehead with a damp handkerchief. Even in the evenings, the D.C. humidity was unbearable in summer. For a man of the Fixer's immense bulk, it was sheer torture.

A waiter with a silver tray hovered nearby. "Excuse me," Jessup said to the passing servant. His hands swooped and came up bearing champagne, a tulip glass of it in each paw. He downed one in a gulp and set the empty glass on a marble credenza. With the other champagne glass in his pudgy hand, he sauntered into the rarified crowd, his sharp eyes carefully noting who was present and, just as important, who was not.

As he passed among the elegantly dressed men and women, he nodded, acknowledged and helloed, his eyes making an inventory of faces with the unremitting logic of a camera. So far he had fourteen senators, three secretaries of state and half a dozen ambassadors. This kind of scene always meant work for him. He spotted a table spread with hors d'oeuvres and made a beeline for it.

He was halfway there when the crowd parted, and the senator who was chairman of the secret House Committee was revealed in his wheelchair, holding court. When he saw Jessup, he stopped the conversation with a wave of his thin hand and excused himself with a generous smile.

The electric motor hummed, and the wheelchair scooted forward, cutting off Jessup's path.

"Another job well done, Walker." The old man smiled with chafed, cracked lips.

"To your credit, I'm sure." Jessup raised his champagne glass in a salute and sipped. He knew the senator was capable of a lot, and in a way admired him for the ability to turn most situations to his advantage and come out on top.

He knew the senator had extracted a favor from the director of the FBI in exchange for the use of the men in Barrabas's secret commando squad. The old pol was a brilliant master of the deal. While he wrapped his rhetoric in sentiments about God, the flag and the American way, the only person he ever went to bat for was himself.

"Terrible tragedy, about the scientist, Young." The senator shook his head sadly. "Terrible."

"Yeah." Jessup downed the second glass of champagne. He could see a river of crocodile tears streaming across the old man's cracked and withered cheeks.

"My boys wanted to keep right on going," the Fixer drawled laconically. His eyes continued to float around the room, and he edged slowly away.

"Well, Jessup," the disabled senator said, grinning. "I'm always ready to give those fine men another assignment. I know they've been busy for the NSA. This Barrabas fellow, he's on quite a winning streak."

"Their skills are for hire, but they cannot be bought," Jessup stated flatly. It was an opinion about the SOBs he had secretly harbored for a long time.

"I've noticed. But it won't last forever. Adios!"

With that, the wheelchair hummed in reverse, changed gears, and the senator rolled back into the crowd.

Ultimately, the decision to use the secret squad was always made in the highest circle of power. But in the past, the senator had been the one man who channeled the covert government assignments to the commandos via Jessup. But the NSA recently had started to rely on the SOBs' services more and more. Despite his run-ins with the commando squad—some of which he'd barely survived—the senator knew there were times when they were the only solution. Therefore, he wasn't totally giving up on their services, though his hatred for Nile Barrabas was no secret. It was he whom the ancient senator blamed—unfairly—for his paralyzed legs.

The butler appeared at Jessup's elbow and dipped with a slight bow. "The telephone, Mr. Jessup. From your office in New York."

The big Texan cast a longing glance in the direction of the food. "Is there a quiet room..."

"Certainly, sir. Come this way."

The din of cocktail conversation faded and was cut off almost entirely when the butler shut the door of the book-lined study and disappeared. The Fixer lifted the phone.

His secretary in New York told him it was Claymore Jeffries. The FBI agent was calling from Salt Lake City, Utah. The secretary put him through to Washington on the conference line.

"What's up?" the Fixer demanded.

"Jessup, you hear about that explosion in the Webber Tunnel in Idaho this morning?"

"A collision, wasn't it? Car with a couple of kids meets truck head-on. All that's left is duck soup?"

Jeffries spoke quickly in a low nervous tone, as if he feared detection. "That's what the media reported because that's what everyone got from witnesses. When the explosion happened, cars were lined up at construction signs at both ends. People swear they saw a road crew, but the Idaho Department of Highways didn't have one working at the tunnel that day. Forensic scientists are studying bone fragments—about all that's left of the people who were in there. So far, they've found that several show signs of bullet damage."

"What was the truck carrying?" Jessup asked quietly.

There was a long pause on the line. "Walker, I could lose my job for telling you this. These details are suddenly highly classified, and for some reason the NSC is breathing down our necks to shut down the case. It was reprocessed waste from a reactor in Washington State, on its way to storage at a desert site in Utah."

"Reprocessed?" Jessup repeated. He felt trouble in the pit of his stomach.

"Yeah," Jeffries's reply was almost reluctant. "It's to separate out the plutonium. What you are left with is—"

"Weapons-grade plutonium," Jessup said flatly.

The technology of reprocessing nuclear waste for pure plutonium had been around for decades but tightly controlled. The waste needed was produced by ordinary atomic power plants located in every country in the world. With knowledge of the secret processes, it was easy for any Third World dictator to acquire plutonium—the necessary ingredient for a nuclear arsenal.

"Plus one missing and presumed dead nuclear scientist," Jessup continued. "Is that what you're implying, Claymore? That the Aryan Nation hijacked this plutonium, that the scientist Young is not really dead but is still their prisoner, and they're going to build a bomb."

"It's just a hunch, Walker. But when things this bizarre happen within a week of each other, my alarms go off. The powers-that-be insist that there is no relationship between the events and it looks to me like the whole case is going to be stonewalled under a blanket of so-called national security considerations."

"Have you got anything for me to look at?"

Suddenly Jeffries's voice changed. He spoke in normal tones, but with a new self-consciousness. "I'll be in Salt Lake City for another day. Can you come out?"

"Yeah."

"Stay at the Marriott. I'll know when to find you." The line went dead.

Jessup's secretary in New York came on the line. "Mr. Jessup?"

"Find an airplane to take me to Salt Lake City tonight. If you have to, charter one. And book me a room at the Marriott."

Jessup arrived in Salt Lake City on a private Lear jet chartered for the occasion. Losing three hours' time from the East Coast, he had flown from sunrise into darkness. As the limousine coasted along an almost deserted expressway toward the city, Jessup rubbed his bleary eyes and peered through the tinted window at the lights downtown, still several miles away.

Forty-eight hours earlier he had been on-site at a farm-house in Amarillo. Today, a clandestine meeting in a Utah hotel. The so-called glamorous life of a free-lance arranger had its tribulations. And none of them had ever helped the Fixer lose weight.

One after the other Jessup threw down the files he held. The first one: Alex "the Greek" Nanos. When Barrabas found him, the muscleman was a busted coast guard veteran working rich women on Miami's Gold Coast. Always a wild card, the Greek was the indispensable fast talker, a skill he also relied on with the ladies. In a fire-fight he had the skilled precision of fine machinery.

The second file: the Greek's best friend, Billy Two, whose full name was William Starfoot II. The six-foot-seven barrel-chested Osage could crush a man's skull with his bare hands. Unfortunately, on the one occasion when Billy Two was a captive, the Russians had fried his brain with intravenous sulfuric acid—liquid fire. Ever since, he had been a little weird about an invisible friend he called Hawk Spirit. Unpredictable, but always reliable, in that when Billy Two felt his presence he seemed to add to his already awesome strength. This so-called ancestral spirit had a much appreciated habit of showing up at the right place at just the right time.

Jessup shook his head skeptically and moved on to the third file: Dr. Leona Hatton, known to all on the team as Lee. A trim dark woman of medium height, her build belied her ability in martial arts. Many men had regretted their assumptions about her being a member of the weaker sex. The daughter of a general, who had lived the society life at one time, she was a fierce and ruthless warrior as well as a trained medical doctor. Most of all, she was respected as an equal by the men.

The fourth file: Claude Hayes. The photograph of the black man stared up at Jessup. Claude had had three or four reincarnations before his most recent one as a soldier of Barrabas. From university leader to Black Panther, to prison gang, then to the Navy and half a dozen liberation wars in Africa, he was the most politically sensitive of the mercenaries, a voice of conscience the others listened to and a man whose advice Barrabas was never unwilling to seek.

The penultimate file: Liam O'Toole. A drunk most of the time, although grudgingly Jessup admitted the man stopped drinking the moment he was on assignment. The loony Irishman was driven by a passion for the bad epic poetry he wrote, and in his civilian life, he was consumed by an obsession to be published. The crusty ex-sergeant had served with Barrabas in Vietnam. Now his blustering personality served to keep the other mercs in line with a minimum amount of resentment.

When it got right down to it, they all respected one another more than anyone else in the world. Perhaps that was why they batted a hundred and lived to tell.

The last file fell in Jessup's lap, and a photograph slipped out. It was in black and white, of a man whose features were so cast in darkness he was almost a silhouette. Behind him were palm trees and a sign in Spanish. He held a Belgian FLN.

It was Barrabas, of course—his build was unmistakable—a photograph taken by an Israeli intelligence agent in South America when the man was fighting a private war.

It was probably the only occasion the old Ranger colonel had banked on the wrong guy. Jessup had pulled him out of a prison hours before his scheduled execution, extracting in return only a promise. As a free-lance intelligence agent and arranger of many things, Jessup had needed a covert action team of highly skilled commandos to execute secret government contracts. Barrabas had promised to lead them.

That was all so long ago. Jessup clicked open his briefcase, stacked the files neatly together, closed it and spun the lock. The limousine slowed for an exit ramp. The buildings of downtown Salt Lake City, bathed in lights, floated on either side of the freeway. A few blocks away, the golden roofs of the famous Mormon Tabernacle spiraled to heaven.

It was a hell of a deal the Vietnam veteran-turned-mercenary accepted, even if his back was to the firing squad wall of a Latin American prison. It amounted to doing the government's dirty work on condition that if the SOBs were caught, captured or killed, it would be in ignominy. The government would deny all knowledge of them.

In foreign countries, it was one thing to work outside the law and exfiltrate, leave forever. But on the rare occasions the mercs became involved in highly secret domestic missions, as covert operators they were also working outside American law. Jessup knew already that the favor Claymore Jeffries was about to ask would put Nile Barrabas and his people in a risky, thankless position.

The limousine slowed under the broad canopy of the Marriott Hotel and the doorman hurried to assist him.

A short while later the burly Texan arrived in his room. He had barely hung up his jacket when there was a light rap on the door. Jessup opened. Claymore Jeffries slipped inside. His briefcase was handcuffed to his wrist.

The FBI man's face was drawn and weary. He had dark bags under his eyes and his suit was rumpled. He set the briefcase on a credenza and detached it from his wrist.

Deftly, he spun the numbers of the combination and opened it.

"The heat was taken off this case too fast after the scientist's remains were found," he told Jessup, removing a manila folder. "The order came from Washington, and when I inquired about it, I was told it was out of my hands. None of the usual follow-up reports or investigation even. A wall of secrecy had been thrown up. I got suspicious."

"Of what?" the Fixer demanded.

"This." Jeffries slipped a document and several eight-by-ten glossy black-and-white photographs from the file folder. "Internal report on that tragedy in the Webber Tunnel a few days ago. Classified. I 'borrowed' it. I could lose my job for this."

Quickly, Walker Jessup scanned the document. He let out a low whistle. "It sure wasn't any accident."

The FBI agent shook his head. "A well-planned and well-executed plutonium hijacking. With one missing, presumed dead nuclear scientist on the books."

"You're implying that those weren't the scientist's remains in the trash compactor in Albuquerque."

"Damn right I am," Jeffries replied. "The only things that identified him were two molars."

"And it's easy enough to pull out molars. You're right, the body could have been anyone's." Jessup flipped the first page of the document. A second sheet listed the final conclusions from the autopsies of the tunnel victims. One of them had been alive when the explosion occurred. The others had been very dead.

"Looks like a bunch of psychos did this," Jessup commented, looking down at the report.

"Very professional, well-trained psychos. One psycho in particular." Jeffries reached out, took one of the photographs from Jessup's hand and placed it on top of the document. "Surveillance stills from the kidnapping at Los Alamos," he explained. "Computer enhanced."

The unretouched photographs were blurry, and most of the men had their heads turned from the camera, or were too far away. The computer-enhanced close-ups showed the faces of four young men.

Jeffries pointed with his index finger to one of them, a tall man with long blond hair.

"He's allegedly a son of Ronald Doule, the major Aryan Nation leader, who was also one of the kidnappers. State records indicate that Doule has no children. But informants have sworn otherwise. However, this is what's important."

Jeffries produced another document from the file and placed it in front of the Fixer. It was a Xerox copy of a police interview from the Webber Tunnel explosion.

"One of the witnesses, a married couple riding in the car that stopped behind the Evans family, positively ID'd this photograph as one of the men in the so-called road crew that stopped traffic. Add up a kidnapped physicist, weapons-grade plutonium and the same perpetrator present at both crimes, and what do you have?"

"If the Aryan Nation is building a nuclear bomb, they'll hold the entire country hostage to their demands," Jessup said.

He folded back the autopsy report. Underneath was the list of Aryan Nation safehouses, farms and compounds stretching from Arizona and Texas to Montana. It was the same list Barrabas and the SOBs had started working on a few days earlier.

The FBI agent's suspicion sounded right to the Fixer. It fit the facts and answered some otherwise inexplicable questions—for instance, why the kidnappers had allowed themselves to be videotaped by surveillance cameras when they seized Young. And why an anonymous phone call tipped off the Albuquerque police on where to find the scientist's compacted remains.

A kidnapping and a hijacking thousands of miles apart had been made to look like completely separate acts, separate enough to throw police bureaucracies into a tizzy and hinder investigations.

The Fixer anticipated Jeffries's next question. "You asking me to have my people continue the search?"

The FBI agent nodded grimly. "With all the stonewalling going on, it's the only way I know to check it out. If I'm right, the country's in trouble."

Jessup paced slowly to the window and looked out over the streetlights floating in the darkness below. It was almost 5:00 a.m. He was exhausted.

"If you're right," the Fixer began slowly, "and the Aryan Nation is building a bomb, what will their demands be?"

"There are members of their organization in federal prisons all over the country serving long sentences for everything from first degree murder of state troopers to racketeering."

"I know all that." Jessup stood with his hands behind his back and looked out the window, unable to disguise the weariness in his voice. "What else?"

"A homeland. They want to create a racially 'pure' national state in the Pacific Northwest."

The Fixer turned around and faced Jeffries again. "You mean, 'Give us Oregon and Washington State or we'll take out New York.'"

The FBI agent shrugged. "Something like that."

Jessup sank into an armchair, still clutching the documents from the manila file folder. He gazed at the list of Posse hideouts, trying to formulate his thoughts.

"There's a problem," he said finally. "A few days ago my people were working covertly but with the secret complicity of high-echelon authorities. They were to carry out lightning-fast raids, and when the local police showed up there was a false trail for them to follow. We even encouraged the belief that an internecine war had broken out among the ranks of the kidnappers."

Jessup stared evenly at Claymore Jeffries. "What you're asking now is for my people to go out on their own to hit the Aryan Nation. That means they're going to have local law enforcement agencies crawling out of the woodwork. My people will be between a rock and a hard place. What if you're wrong and they end up charged with murder, or killed in a shoot-out not with these maniacs but with the police?"

The FBI agent strode to the chair and leaned over the fat man to look him directly in the eyes. "And what if I'm right?"

There was a long silence between the two men.

"We've got to stop them before the bomb is built," Jeffries said firmly. "Not after."

The Fixer nodded. He waved the manila folder in the air. "It's not my decision anymore. It's up to Barrabas and the others."

A look of immense relief broke across Jeffries's tired face.

Jessup handed him back the file. "All I can do is ask."

**6**

Casey Wiggins, Rock Springs' real estate agent, poured out steaming hot mugs of coffee and passed them to her parents. This was their second cup of the day—she had dropped off her two older children at school and the toddler at her nursery—and now had a few minutes' leisure to share.

Ever since her husband, Derek, had walked out, she had been living with her parents. It wasn't easy being a single parent, and she had decided early on to take advantage of her parents' help. They did not need to take care of the children all day, but were immensely helpful and made a huge difference in creating a real home. There was time, this way, for homemaking and a real sense of family. Thank goodness, Casey thought affectionately, that they gave her solid support without trying to run her life.

She fumed sometimes when she thought of her ex and the brazen hussy of a secretary he had moved in with. On the other hand, force of circumstance had motivated her to get her real estate license. In the past two years she had become so successful that she was expecting Derek to file for alimony any day. The financial rewards also allowed all of them to live in a very comfortable and roomy house, which went a long way toward making the arrangement totally harmonious. Privacy was important, after all, she concluded, and turned to her mother with an affectionate look in her eyes.

"Mom, I'll need to be out later today. Some client who can only view a property at a later time, and I think he also wants to take me to dinner after, to compensate for the late hours, I guess," Casey said with a twinge of a smile.

"Isn't that a nice man, dear, but I daresay he doesn't just want to compensate you," the youthful-looking dark-haired woman said to her daughter. "No, I'd imagine he likes you and wants to get to know you better. Just don't worry about hurrying home." She paused to drink some of her coffee, then turned to her husband, who had started to immerse himself in the paper. "Bert, are we still playing bridge this afternoon with the Kettlewells?"

He peered at her over his glasses and lowered his paper. "Yes, Mary, the rubber is still on. And it's time we win— don't go making those impossible bids now, or we will have one more fiasco on our hands." Then the handsome gray-haired man laughed at his wife's crestfallen face and added, "But I swear that when it comes to actual play, you are the best!" He reached over to squeeze her hand warmly.

Casey just started to offer some of the bran muffins sitting on the table when she heard the screen door at the front of the house slam shut and turned to look down the hallway. A tall blond man in a dark jacket stood at the door. Beside him was another young man, in olive drab fatigues.

"Can I help you?" Casey called out, but she had already put the plate down and was striding toward the front door, annoyed by their audacity at walking in uninvited, but not otherwise alarmed. Rock Springs, Wyoming was not by nature a suspicious or dangerous town.

Sonny Doule sauntered down the hallway, the heels of his boots tapping heavily on the polished hardwood floor. There was something odd about the wide smile on his tanned face. Casey backed up slightly as he came nearer, and cast a glance behind her as though wanting to call her father. She heard the scraping of chairs from the kitchen and realized he was coming to investigate who the visitors were.

"Someone at your office told us where to find you."

"What do you want?" Casey demanded sharply.

"A man came to see you yesterday. Tall. White hair but not old. Big strong guy." His words hissed slightly between the gap in his teeth.

Something told Casey all was not well. She slowly retreated toward the kitchen and almost bumped into her father at the doorway. He put out a hand to steady her and looked inquiringly at the strangers.

"Why do you need to know?" she asked, hoping to be rid of them. Now she felt real fear when she noted that the slightly insane-looking smile was still stretched tight across the man's face. And there was a hunger in his eyes, but it was not sexual; it was something else, something scary that she could not even name.

Her father drew himself up to his full height by her side and turned a stern look at the men. "What for? Who are you, anyway? You have no right to barge in—"

With no warning, Sonny smashed Bert Wiggins across the face with the back of his hand, knocking him back into the kitchen, where he staggered to the floor in a daze. With a terrified expression, Mary rushed to help her husband. She looked up at the young man from her crouched position on the floor with an unbelieving look of utter panic.

Sonny withdrew his Luger. From another pocket he took out a silencer and efficiently screwed it to the barrel of the gun.

"Please leave us alone," Casey screamed and flattened herself against the wall.

Her father was scrambling to get up from the floor, with his wife holding hysterically on to his arm to try and keep him back. "No, Bert, no!" she begged.

He shook her off, and while Sonny looked on with a cool amused expression, launched himself at the blond young man. He was halfway through the kitchen when Sonny's gun coughed once. Bert's face disappeared.

Sonny looked at Casey. "Just want to know where I can find a tall man with almost white hair. I saw him walk out of your place." He pointed the weapon at Mary, who was looking at the remains of her husband in an absolute transport of white-faced agony and terror.

"His name is Barrabas," Casey said quickly, her voice hardly coming out. "Nile Barrabas. He's selling his ranch. The side road off Highway 191, ten miles past 220." Casey extended her hand protectively toward her mother and dead father.

Sonny smiled wide. The gun coughed again, and Mary spun about in a spray of high-pressure blood that hosed the room.

Casey let out an anguished sound of inhuman pain and fear. She was immobile, frozen with shock. Then she became mute, having somehow remembered to be thankful that her children were out of the house. She knew they would be orphans, but at least they would live on. She turned toward Sonny, and could not make a sound even when he leveled his weapon at her. The Luger spit its bullet from close range, and a great red blot began to spread on her white linen jacket.

Sonny stood looking down at her in silence, then decisively dispatched another slug into her dying body.

Chuka, who was right behind him, looked over the blond man's shoulder. "Jesus, Sonny, look at this mess."

"Well, we want a revolution," Sonny remarked happily, "and there ain't no halfway measures." He stuck the gun back inside his jacket and started walking down the hallway toward the front door. "A ranch out on Highway 191. Now that I know where he's at, I got something real special I wanna show him!"

A few minutes later, Sonny and Chuka pulled up beside a telephone booth on a gas station lot several blocks from the Wigginses' residence. Sonny honked. Spiker was on the phone. He waved quickly and turned back to his conversation. His face registered surprise, and he hung up. He burst out the door and sprinted for the van.

"That reporter, Bill Stead. I phoned every goddamn hotel in town. He's at the Holiday Inn and he just checked out."

Spiker jumped inside the van. "Guy at the desk said he just paid his bill and went to collect his car in the underground garage. If we hurry, we can catch him there!"

Sonny hit the gas and pulled into traffic. The hotel was downtown, a high rise of nine stories that towered over everything else in Rock Springs.

It took them barely a minute to get to the entrance to the parking garage. Sonny turned in, rolling down his window as an attendant stepped to the door of his booth. The blond man raised his Luger and fired. The guard's forehead split open and he popped back into the booth, disappearing from sight.

Sonny hit the gas again, and the van squealed around a corner onto the first level of parked cars.

"There he is!" Chuka shouted.

Bill Stead slammed the rear door of the station wagon, and stepped around to the passenger side to get in. The cameraman stood by the driver's door, pulling the key from the lock. Both men looked up. The van screeched to a halt, blocking the network car. Chuka jumped from the van.

The cameraman threw himself at the punk, his fists flailing and an uppercut landing solidly on Chuka's chin.

From the door of the van, Sonny fired a 3-round burst from a silenced MAC-10. It sputtered and the cameraman dropped.

Bill Stead bolted for the narrow opening between the fenders of the two vehicles, when suddenly the rear doors of the van were flung open. Spiker jumped down, grabbing the anchorman in a headlock.

Sonny, casual as always, climbed from the van, sauntered over and took charge.

"Search the car," he told Spiker, nodding toward the white station wagon with the network logo on the door panels.

Sonny grabbed Bill Stead by the throat, his strong fingers sinking into the neck on either side of his trachea. Stead squirmed, his eyes white with fear.

"You won't get away—" he gasped, and his words were choked off as Sonny dug his fingers into his flesh.

"All I want," the blond man said slowly, staring hard into the reporter's frightened eyes, "is the videocassette from yesterday."

Stead managed to shake his head slightly, despite the punk's grip on his neck. He felt the hand at his throat relax slightly.

"Can't," he managed to say hoarsely. The steel fingers clawed deeper. Screams welled in his chest but came out as tiny, almost inaudible sounds. He realized he was whimpering.

"You pathetic bastard," Sonny said succinctly.

Chuka and Spiker threw the suitcases from the Plymouth and dumped them open on the concrete floor. Quickly, the parking space was covered with clothing, personal objects and smashed video equipment. Spiker kicked everything about in search for the videocassette, while Chuka cut away at the car seats with a long knife.

Spiker found a polished aluminum case in the trunk. He shot the lock off and dumped out several dozen cassettes.

"Which one is it!" Sonny demanded from Stead. The anchorman shook his head cringing. The hands at his throat loosened.

"That man has it!" Stead cried weakly. "Barrabas. The one with the white hair."

Sonny's hands tightened around Stead's neck again. He forced the television reporter to his knees and let go of him.

"You sure about that?"

Stead nodded as best he could.

"Well, we know where to find him now, don't we."

Sonny swung his Luger and pistol-whipped Stead across the face.

Stead's jaw snapped. He fell over the hood of an adjacent car, clutching his head with his hands and moaning terribly. Blood poured from his mouth and his face looked distorted.

Sonny jumped over the car and grabbed him again. He put his hands around Stead's neck and pressed both thumbs into his trachea again, cutting off the flow of oxygen to his lungs.

Stead looked up at him, startled, his face turning red with the growing awareness that he was being strangled to death. He stiffened, his fingernails digging into Sonny's enclosing hands, making them bleed. Desperately Stead tried to disengage the murdering grip.

It was as Bill Stead realized that he was going to die that his eyes lowered and he saw the bright yellow drum with the radiation warning sign in the back of the blue van.

Sonny saw the direction of Stead's gaze and understood that the man had made the connection. He let go. Stead fell facefirst. He pushed himself to his knees, clawing at his destroyed throat.

"Plutonium, Mr. Teevee Reporter," Sonny boomed. "Hijacked from the truck in the Webber Tunnel. They didn't tell America that on the news, did they? Well, it wasn't an accident. It was us. Your greatest scoop ever. Let me give you another one. That nuclear scientist from Los Alamos? He's alive, too."

Sonny stepped back and kicked Stead in the stomach, knocking him over. The man's chest sank, like air deflating from a child's inflatable toy. Then he was still. He lay on his knees, his face against the oil spot on the concrete floor.

"It could've been the story of a lifetime, Mr. Teevee Reporter. Too bad you won't live to be famous."

Bill Stead stared, his eyes as cold and white as marbles.

Barrabas had finished packing most of what he wanted from the house and carrying it out to the Bronco. The For Sale signs had been nailed along the fence that faced the road. When he drove out for the last time, everything else was up to the realtor.

He geared up for the final farewell, to close the last page on a long-finished chapter of his life. He picked up the videocassette he had taken from Bill Stead a day earlier and debated where to pack it. There was an old television in the house, but no VCR. He wanted Jessup to see the tape before he returned it to the television network.

The telephone rang. It was Doris Amberton. "I heard you were selling out," she said.

"So soon?"

"Sure. Half my customers last night had driven past your property and seen the signs up. You should know people around here got nothing better to talk about."

"Well, I can't take care of the place," Barrabas told her. "It's time to let go of it."

"Is there any possibility we might have a couple of hours together before you drive off? For old times' sake."

It took the colonel only a few seconds to accept. "Sure." He laughed gently. "I got nothing pressing except a long drive to Cheyenne."

Several minutes later, he climbed into the red four-wheeler and sped down the road to the highway, not bothering to close the gate behind him.

Half a mile away, where Highway 191 wound over the crest of a hill, Sonny sat in the passenger seat of the blue van, watching through binoculars the Bronco disappear, and the dust on the road settle in its tracks.

"Perfect," he murmured.

"What's happening?" Chuka asked from the driver's seat.

"He's going somewhere."

"Well, what are we supposed to do, follow him or sit here and wait? People are expecting us in Arkansas this afternoon. You know how pissed your old man gets when—"

"Shut up, Chuka," Sonny snapped. "I want that videocassette back."

"Yeah, but how do you know he doesn't have it with—"

"Just drive down there," Sonny ordered. "I got something special in mind for this asshole. I'm going to wipe him clean off the face of the earth."

Chuka did as he was ordered, and a minute later the van pulled up in front of the old farmhouse.

"How d'ya know there ain't someone else out here?" Spiker asked as the young man exited their vehicle. His voice was strangely hushed as if he was afraid he might be overheard. He jammed a new mag into his auto.

Sonny waved his MAC-10. "I got insurance," he leered. "Now just get the plastic out." He grinned broadly. "And wire the place for sound."

A steady westerly wind flowed across the wide open rangeland, bringing a hint of chill from the high mountain passes. They heard grass rustling, and a whiny creak from an old hinge somewhere, but the property looked deserted.

Chuka looked around carefully, observing the outbuildings and the weathered frame house. A crumbling porch ran across the front, and a rusting television antenna leaned awkwardly at the peak of the roof.

"No basement," he said, noting that the old farmhouse stood on foot-high pylons. "That'll make it easy." He opened the back door of the van and grabbed two square canvas haversacks, clearly stamped with U.S. Army markings. They were heavy. He dumped them on the ground and reached inside for a metal toolbox.

"Spiker, give me a hand. I'll check out the inside."

Sonny strode fearlessly up the steps and across the porch. He tested the doorknob. The door wasn't even locked. Without hesitating, he kicked it open and went inside.

The interior was simple, a living room with doors leading straight through to a small dining room and then the kitchen. More doorways along one side led to bedrooms. Sonny noticed almost immediately the suitcases standing next to the front door. The expensive leather bags contrasted strangely with the frayed condition of the furniture.

"Damn," he muttered. It looked as if his quarry was about to pull out. That could complicate things. Then he noticed the videocassette lying on a nearby table. His eyes lit up. He took it and walked back outside.

Chuka had the haversacks open and sixteen two-and-a-half-pound blocks of C-4 laid neatly on the ground. The acrid smell lingered in the air despite the steady breeze. Striker busied himself by screwing grooved priming adapters into the threaded cap wells.

Sonny held up the cassette. "I got what I wanted."

"Half of it, anyway." Chuka grinned, looking up from his work. "Soon's we get this done, you'll have the other half of what you want."

The blond man threw the cassette into the van. "We got a problem. This guy's got his bags packed and is ready to roll. How we going to set it up so's—"

"We'll figure something," Chuka cut in. "Give me a hand with the detonating cord." He motioned toward a nearby roll of braided cotton tube filled with PETN, a powerful military explosive. Busily screwing adapters into the blocks of C-4, he added with a grin, "It burns with a velocity rate of 21,000 feet a second. He'll never even know."

Sonny grabbed the roll. "Oh yeah? Is there some way we can do it so he does know?"

"We'll think of something," he repeated with a little laugh. He liked this kind of job, and he was very good at it.

Working quickly, Chuka placed the explosives underneath the house, hiding them behind the short posts that held the building off the ground. Sonny and Spiker quickly strung the C-4 together, encircling the house with the PETN cord. The three young men came together inside the house.

"We don't have no pressure release detonator," Chuka told them, eyeing different items in the room. "Otherwise we could just put one under one of those suitcases."

Sonny snapped his fingers. "I got it!"

He strode to the television and turned it on. The set hummed before the screen sprang to life. The picture rolled, then was steady, but snowy.

"Hook it up to this. So when it's turned off, it detonates." His eyes burned with a joyous intensity. "He'll wonder how it got turned on. Then he'll turn it off before he leaves."

IT WAS LATE AFTERNOON when Jessup drove up to Barrabas's house in the rented Buick. The drive from Salt Lake City was only two hours, but after sleeping a few hours, he had spent the better part of the day agonizing over what to say.

A storm brewed in the east, faint rumblings of thunder barely audible, yet growing louder. The sky was low with brooding clouds and the wind was picking up, moist with the smell of rain. Jessup parked the car a hundred feet from the house and lumbered across the gravel drive, half expecting a dog to scramble around a corner barking, or the man himself come to the veranda to greet him. Instead, the place looked strangely deserted. There weren't even any cars.

Thunder growled much closer. The light turned faintly purple and objects looked hyperreal, like two-dimensional surfaces erected as backdrops. The wind was starting to spit. Leaning heavily on his cane, Jessup climbed the steps to the veranda.

A strange metallic odor made him stop and sniff the air. It seemed familiar, but the strong breezes blowing down from the mountains wafted it away before he was able to identify it. He tried the front door. It was open.

The moment he went inside he felt relief. A couple of suitcases were stacked by the door. Barrabas was here.

He called. His voice echoed through the shabby house but went unanswered. He stepped tentatively through the living room, peering into the kitchen and bedrooms. No one was home.

The television in the living room blared a basketball game. For no particular reason, it somehow seemed uncharacteristic of Nile Barrabas to leave on the TV and go out. But the colonel's Wyoming experiences were unknown to the Fixer, and he knew that people sometimes reverted to old habits when they stepped back into the environment they grew up in.

Feeling uncomfortable in an empty, unfamiliar house, Jessup debated for a moment his next course of action and decided to wait in the car. He reached to turn the television off when he heard the sound of a vehicle approaching from the highway.

Stepping to the window, he saw a red Bronco come to a stop at the end of the gravel, twenty feet from the house. Barrabas was at the wheel, a woman beside him. Jessup watched them talk a moment while the engine died. Then he hurried to the front porch to greet them.

Barrabas was startled for an instant until he recognized the man walking from his house.

"I thought your car belonged to the real estate agent," Barrabas shouted, walking around the cab to open Doris's door. The woman stepped out. Her beauty, what with the streak of pure white hair running through the jet-black, and the classic features, was quite awesome.

Jessup lumbered down the steps toward them.

"A friend's stopped by," Barrabas explained to Doris, making introductions. "Very unexpectedly."

"In the neighborhood? Just dropped in?" Doris asked with light sarcasm, her eyebrows rising in mock doubt. She smiled at Barrabas. "Or is it business? I'll go inside and make coffee, while you talk."

Graciously, Doris walked toward the house. The colonel looked at the fat man. They waited until she had gone inside.

"Doris and I go back a long way," Barrabas commented with a broad grin.

"I'd say you should make up for lost time."

"I appreciate that, Jessup, but there's always a down side to you showing up. Otherwise I'd say I was glad to see you."

Doris noticed a strange odor when she crossed the porch and entered the old farmhouse. She associated it with the length of time the house had been empty.

She walked through the living room slowly, taking in the old house that she hadn't been inside of for years. It was stepping into the past, like a tourist seeing something carefully preserved in a little-visited corner of an obscure museum, stale, dusty and locked behind glass. She understood Nile's reasons for selling out. If she had any place to run away to, or anything to sell, she'd do exactly the same.

Suddenly she felt weak, and she couldn't tell whether it was nostalgia or regret that she was feeling. She sat on the ancient overstuffed chesterfield, her hands holding her fluttery stomach. She fought back the flow of tears.

As a teenager she had learned what it was like to be os-
tracized, from the moment of her sexual awakening. Early
on she had shrugged her shoulders at what other people
talked about. They said she was a bad girl, the fast kind.
And she supposed it was true.

But then she remembered the ecstasy she had known on
sultry summer nights with a boy in the cab of a pickup, or
in the back seat of a Nash, and how much she really had
been in love—with both Jake and Nile, but Nile a little
more, maybe because there was something about him that
she was never allowed to understand. Or have.

Jake was always ready to surrender to her, and when
Nile left, she finally accepted. They ran away when they
were seventeen. All three of them.

A few hours earlier that afternoon she and Barrabas had
made love again, for the first time in years, and the chem-
istry was still there between them. That was why this was
all coming back to her. She remembered what being
seventeen was like, a little. When they were finished, she
had told Nile he was even better now.

He had smiled long and hard at that. Then they did it
again. The second time she let her eyes wander across his
body, counting all the scars that marked his flesh, and
wondering if she really wanted to know the story each one
told. Finally she decided in favor of the moment, instead
of the past.

Doris felt calmer now with the pleasant memories, and
remembered that her mission was to make coffee. She
stood, glancing out the living room window. Nile and his
friend were walking toward the Buick. She knew it was
business. Something of whatever he did, which she assumed to be undercover stuff of some kind, but it was
something he didn't talk about.

Then it hit her. He would be going away now. So soon. She felt the queasiness in her stomach again, but this time fought it. They had returned to the farm for his suitcases, so he could stay a couple of extra days at her place. She knew it was just a fling and she'd be brokenhearted for a week or two after he left, but damned if she wasn't going to make the most of it now.

She steeled herself, telling herself she didn't care, and didn't want to know. Make coffee, she decided. It was a conditioned response, a chore disguising the brutality of the moment. She started across the living room for the kitchen, passing the television with barely a glance. When the percolator was on the stove, she returned to the living room.

Through the window she saw Barrabas and Jessup, still standing beside the Buick. The TV blared a noisy sports program. Doris turned around. It was basketball. She wondered if, romance aside, Nile was anything like Jake. Her ex-husband used to walk in the door, grab a beer and head straight for the living room to watch baseball. She hated competing for attention with a television set.

Doris decided to turn it off.

JESSUP AND BARRABAS WALKED toward the Buick while Jessup explained the reason for his visit.

"So Jeffries thinks the Aryan Nation have thrown up an elaborate smoke screen to give themselves time to build a nuclear bomb," Barrabas summed up when they reached the car.

The rain was holding off, although the sky to the east was dark with clouds. Occasionally the wind whipped a few stray drops of rain past.

"Force the scientist, Young, to build it, anyway," Jessup added.

"It makes sense. Especially with the inside story on that tunnel explosion.'

"The thing is, Jeffries wants you to get involved. You and the other SOBs. On a pro bono basis. He's given me all the information you need to start."

Barrabas stopped and scratched his head, looking into the wind. "The question is, can he hold off the law enforcement agencies while we do what's necessary."

Jessup shook his head. "No, he can't."

Barrabas growled. "Then what's he wasting my time for? Let's have a look at what he gave you."

"My pleasure." Jessup rubbed his hands together and reached inside the car for his briefcase. He handed the manila folder to Barrabas. "The list of known safehouses, and this."

Jessup flipped the folder open and pulled out the photographs. "A sampling of who you might run into. Suspected Posse members. Computer-enhanced stills from the videotape of the kidnapping at Los Alamos. Apparently the blond one was ID'd at the site of the Webber Tunnel explosion and the plutonium robbery."

Barrabas stared at the grainy blowup of Sonny's face. He was executing one of the guards, who knelt before him in a posture of submission.

"This one—" Barrabas pointed.

"Yeah, he's supposed to be a real psycho," Jessup drawled.

"He was in town yesterday. In Rock Springs. I got a bone to pick with him."

Jessup's eyes grew large. He reached across Barrabas and flipped several pages over to another page. "Read all about him."

Barrabas quickly scanned the document. It gave all the information known about the kidnapper—including the information that he was alleged to be a son of the Posse leader, Ronald Doule.

Jessup shifted impatiently. The wind was picking up again, and he shivered. He wanted to go inside, but for some reason was afraid to suggest it.

"You watching the basketball game?" he finally asked.

Barrabas looked up from the list. "Basketball?"

"On TV inside." Jessup gestured toward the house by tilting his head in that direction.

Barrabas looked up. "The TV was on?" he asked sharply.

Jessup nodded. He saw the look on Barrabas's face and remembered the strange acrid smell on the porch of the house. Suddenly he knew what it was. Plastics.

"Oh my God!" He turned white.

A split second later the frame house quivered and trembled. Then it began to disintegrate, the roof turning soft and lifting up, while the walls wavered and fell outward. Then everything shattered. The concussion wave hit Jessup and Barrabas, then the sound of the explosion deafened them, battering their ears.

The men slammed into each other and fell into a heap. Barrabas flung himself across the Fixer, pinning him down and burying his face in the fat man's back. Debris rained down, shards of wood and bits of plaster battering them, until the two men were covered. Slowly the fragments stopped falling.

Barrabas and Jessup pushed themselves apart. Barrabas saw Jessup speaking to him but he couldn't hear. His ears rang from the concussion. He motioned with his hands and Jessup nodded.

They were covered in dust and bits of rubble. The house had completely disappeared, and the red Bronco was a scorched, smoking hulk. The debris was scattered about thickly and in tiny pieces in a radius of several hundred feet. Small fires dotted the landscape.

Barrabas staggered forward, uncertain of where to look. He was covered with dust and tiny splinters of wood. Thunder boomed overhead, and suddenly the skies opened, torrents of rain pelting down. They were drenched within seconds, the dust on their faces congealing and running down their cheeks like dirty tears.

Barrabas forced himself to go on, one step at a time, looking for Doris but not wanting to find her, wanting to believe in miracles, but knowing that life had its own cold logic.

Barrabas saw it, not far from what was left of the foundations. What remained wasn't even human.

In an instant, Barrabas had no doubts whatsoever about who was responsible. The blond man who was thought to be Ronald Doule's son. A bunch of crazy fanatics who were building a nuclear bomb.

Claymore Jeffries didn't have to ask.

Now it was personal.

7

Jake Larraby lived in the badlands, in a little rundown trailer he'd hauled to the foot of a mesa years earlier. It was out in the Uinta Mountains, six miles south of Rock Springs, and not far from the Utah border. Hidden on top of a rocky hill in the shadows of the immense column of eroded rusty-red rock, it was further concealed by sagebrush that he had carefully planted along one side.

Behind it was a long narrow corral and a small outbuilding where he kept two horses and parked the four-wheel drive that took him across four and a half miles of near-impassible terrain to the state highway. He called it, jokingly, his Fortress of Solitude, a name inspired by the Antarctic refuge of a caped superhero of comic book fame. There was a gasoline generator that provided electricity, and for water a shaft deep into an artesian well that ran beneath the mountain range.

It had rained most of the night, easing the heat of the relentless sunlight that baked the badlands and cooling the light winds bouncing off the Rockies to the west. The sky was clear and blue, with an occasional popcorn cloud. By just past noon the day after the killings, the world looked innocent again.

Barrabas waited patiently inside the trailer, his eyes fixed on the rutted trail that led from civilization to the hill below. Earlier that morning, Jessup and Larraby had gone into Rock Springs to visit the sheriff. Both prevailed upon Barrabas to stay behind the scenes until they figured out what was going on. The town had gone crazy with the massacre of the Wiggins family, and the body found at Barrabas's dynamited ranch house.

They left him behind to fight the temptation to single-handedly launch his own fierce retribution on the men who'd booby-trapped his house and killed the innocent woman.

His face was bruised, and there was a long cut on one cheek. It was shallow, looking worse than it was. His back, however, was purple from the torrent of debris that had rained down, and it was painful and stiff when he moved.

Three times in the past hour he had disassembled his Browning HP, cleaned it, oiled it and put it back together. More than anything he wanted to use it.

Doris Amberton had been dead almost eighteen hours.

Finally he heard the engine of an approaching vehicle and his wait was over. Larraby's black Cherokee Jeep rumbled around the side of the mesa and lurched to a halt at the bottom of the hill. The lanky cowboy stepped down from the driver's side, while Walker Jessup exited the other side, and plodded uphill across the rocky ground.

By the time the Fixer reached the trailer, he was huffing and puffing, and heaving his massive bulk around as though it was a flour sack he couldn't carry another moment. For Jake, it was a Sunday stroll. But the man's weathered brown face was grim.

Jessup banged his ubiquitous briefcase onto the table beside Barrabas's gun and collapsed onto a banquette with frayed cushions. He was too winded to even think of mopping his forehead. Larraby sat slowly in an old wooden chair across the table from Barrabas.

"Officially you're dead," the cowboy told him. "Killed in the explosion at your house. The sheriff owes me a few, so he'll sit on it for a few days. But eventually he'll have to identify the remains as Doris's."

Jake stopped and swallowed, and Barrabas didn't miss the moisture glistening in his eyes. The aging cowboy swallowed again, steeling himself against the tug and pull of anger and emotion.

"I don't trust that deputy of his, though, what's-his-name, Smithby," he muttered.

"Why not?" Jessup demanded, fanning his jowly red face with a magazine and breathing audibly.

"Aryan Nation," Jake answered. "You never know who is and who ain't. Like I told you, they believe the sheriff of the county should be the law of the land. And there are more in their back pocket than they got hogs in Iowa."

Jessup tucked the handkerchief into his breast pocket and turned to face Barrabas. "The big news is that Bill Stead was attacked, too. They left him for dead in the underground parking lot beneath his hotel. They crushed his trachea, but a hotel employee found him and resuscitated him. Then the ambulance got there and paramedics stuck a respirator down his throat. He died an hour ago in the hospital, with hemorrhage as the immediate cause of death. It was apparently the aftereffect of being pistol-whipped. We went to see him, and just in the nick of time too, as it turned out.

"It was obvious he was going to die, no matter what. We managed to ask him a couple of questions before he went." Jessup snapped open his briefcase and removed the file folder. He let the photographs of the Los Alamos kidnapping fall on the table.

"First, he ID'd the blonde in these pictures, the one who's allegedly Doule's son, as one of the men who attacked him."

Jake Larraby took the second photograph and looked at it carefully. Almost absentmindedly the aging cowboy continued the story. "We asked him if he knew anything about plutonium. He was pretty weak and couldn't talk, but he nodded his head."

"Then I asked if he'd seen it with the blond man in the photo when he was beaten," Jessup picked up the story. "He nodded yes again."

Jake Larraby was staring intently at the photograph of Sonny Doule. He held it closer to the light and squinted. "I know I saw this one up in Utah."

Jessup and Barrabas looked at him quizzically.

Jake nodded to them. "I knew soon as I saw this yesterday that I'd seen the young feller around somewhere. I've been racking my brain ever since then. Now I remember. It's up in Utah. I saw him around a ranch there. Way up in the hills north of Great Salt Lake."

"You're sure?" Barrabas demanded.

Jake nodded. "Of course I'm sure. The reason the feds can't get a handle on this guy is because he's a sovereign. They don't know he exists. No birth certificates, no schooling. There's hundreds of them been raised that way on isolated ranches all over the West for the past two decades. But I saw him. I know it."

The Fixer shuffled through some spec sheets until he found the list of Aryan Nation safehouses. He tapped his finger at one entry, an isolated mountainside ranch in northern Utah.

"Here?"

Larraby read the typed print slowly and nodded.

"It's halfway up the side of a mountain where it has a view of the entire valley and all the approaches below. Like a goddamn fortress, and it's no accident they built it that way. There are a lot of stories in that part of the country. Some of the old settlers still cling to polygamy. The men set themselves up like biblical patriarchs. They don't like having outsiders nosing around up there. People have been known to disappear."

"Then that's where we'll hit first," Barrabas said.

Jessup and Larraby exchanged glances.

"I'm with you, Nile," Jake said.

A moment of silence fell between the men, broken finally by Jessup. "Where are the boys?" he asked Barrabas.

The colonel gazed out the window to the vast emptiness of the badlands, unable to tear his thoughts away from Doris Amberton, Casey Wiggins and her unfortunate parents, victims every one of them of an arbitrary maniac.

"Last I heard O'Toole was heading for Los Angeles to sell his latest epic," Barrabas told Jessup. "Nanos, Hayes and Starfoot are in Miami, supposedly to sportfish, but I heard some talk about them taking out a crack house for the hell of it. Lee's in Boston."

"Round them up?" Jessup asked.

Barrabas nodded in the affirmative. "Round them up."

EVENING TWILIGHT in Arkansas lent a weird dark glow to the forested hills and winding highways.

Sonny, Chuka and Spiker took turns at the wheel of the blue van, transporting the stolen plutonium across state lines from Wyoming through Colorado to Arkansas. Several times, for long stretches of country highway, they found themselves carefully escorted by a state trooper or a county sheriff, an ally of the Aryan Nation who had been alerted to the special shipment.

A thousand miles from Rock Springs, Wyoming, Sonny turned off the highway onto a gravel road that led between a dip in two low mountains. Craggy limestone bluffs rose on each side, and pine trees climbed the rock, their gnarled roots clutching fiercely at the thin soil.

Sonny flicked the headlights once. A thousand feet away, hidden by trees on the bluffs overlooking the road, a man looked through an image-intensifying night-vision scope mounted to his rifle. The barrel of the rifle moved slowly in line with the passing vehicle. Then he dropped it and spoke into the tiny transmitter of the radio strapped to his right shoulder.

The engine moaned in complaint as Sonny fed it gas, and finally roared uphill until they reached a level stretch. The road twisted sharply, and then turned again, so that suddenly the van broke into the open and the road headed straight down into a wide green valley.

The forests lining the sides were masses of darkness in the twilight, but rocks glowed white in the wide open fields that lined the bottom of the valley, and outcroppings of gray limestone on the shaggy hillsides shone pink from the sun setting opposite.

The western sky was a diminishing red, while darkness filled the east like ink spreading into water. Only the dim glow of light through windows across the valley distinguished the farmhouse from the shadows of the limestone bluffs that towered above it.

"We made it." Chuka rolled down the window and spit.

The van lurched and bounced over gravel, and slowly accelerated. At the bottom of the valley, he turned onto a secondary gravel road, so narrow it was impossible to pass another car. Almost instantly, blinding headlights were reflected in the window mirror. They dimmed. A Jeep was following them.

The sky lost what was left of daylight, and the forest on either side of the road grew into an indistinguishable mass. At another crossroad, a second Jeep pulled into line. A mile later Sonny braked at a driveway leading off the road. He turned off his headlights and steered left.

They rolled up to a steel gate and stopped. Movements in the blackness at the side of the road took shape, becoming men with rifles.

The gate swung slightly open, and more men came out of a small guard post on the other side. The two Jeeps pulled in behind and parked side by side.

Sonny rolled down his window, letting in the loud chirping of crickets. The night was damp and still warm. Car doors slammed, and bolts clicked on rifles. A dozen men milled in the darkness beyond the van.

"Bones in, bones out." Sonny Doule spoke from the window.

"Sonny? You finally here?" The face that appeared beside the van belonged to Sam Shane, an older man with gray hair and a grizzled face.

Formerly a Kansas farmer, Shane had lost the family farm to a local bank in a foreclosure on a loan. Down and out at the age of fifty, he was introduced by a neighbor to people who told him it wasn't his fault that he lost the farm. They had some pretty clear ideas who was to blame—the Federal Reserve Bank, the blacks, the Jews, eastern capitalists, even the President of the United States.

Now he was a soldier of the Aryan Nation, dedicated to the noble cause.

"You're a day overdue and your father's fit to be tied," he told Sonny.

"I'll take care of him," the blond man said confidently.

Shane stood back and waved his arm at his men. Two of them swung the gate wide open. Yet another Jeep pulled out from behind the guardhouse and waited for the van to fall in behind.

With military precision the cavalcade fell into place and moved through the gates, a procession of red and amber parking lights clustered on the road heading to the top of the hill.

In the farmhouse, Ronald Doule, Sr., heard vehicles approach and knew that Sonny had finally arrived. He walked to the front porch of the rambling, two-story frame house. The glow of headlights shimmered on the treetops along the road as it wound its way up the hill.

He turned to the wiry man with sandy-brown hair who stood nearby. Keith Rotsky was a brother to Duane Rotsky, who had been killed in the house in Amarillo. His Aryan Nation colleagues called him, only half-joking, the Field Marshal—after Göring, Hitler's chief of staff.

"Let's get the crew rolling."

At the front of the house, men were waiting with lights and video cameras. The cavalcade of vehicles paraded in a circle, with the blue van coming to a stop beside the steps to the porch.

Spiker opened up the rear doors and jumped out to a chorus of cheers.

"Back it up!" a man yelled, motioning with his arm.

Sonny put the gears into reverse and backed away from the house. He braked, grabbed his knapsack and stepped out to a beam of blinding white light. Two men held portable lights, and shone them in the open back door of the van. The yellow lead container was brilliantly illuminated, and the man with the camcorder moved in for a close-up.

Ronald Doule, Sr., broke through the crowd of men. "Sonny!" he called sharply to his son. The young man left the crowd of men and joined his father. Doule, Sr., turned without saying a word and stalked back toward the house.

Sonny sighed with exaggerated exasperation. Reluctantly he followed.

Barely inside the front door, Doule about-turned to face Sonny. The young man's face was bruised and raw from the beating Barrabas had given him, and a right upper incisor was missing.

"You're almost a day late."

"We had some business to attend to on the way."

"In Rock Springs, Wyoming, by any chance?" Ronald Doule, Sr.'s face darkened with anger. "What the hell are you taking chances with? Why's your face all battered up like that?"

At first Sonny was taken aback by his father's knowledge of the incident. "Some sheriff talk to you?" he asked, with a touch of insolence. Air whistled through the gap of his missing tooth.

"I seen it on the TV news since first thing this morning!" Doule, Sr., growled. "And Smithby, the deputy sheriff in Rock Springs, phoned. A hell of a bloodbath. What happened? That TV reporter see you?"

Sonny nodded. "Who they say did it?"

"They say they don't know. Escaped convicts possibly, but they don't rule out a vendetta. Who was this guy Barrabas?"

A smile appeared from ear to ear on Sonny's face. "A dumb farmer who got in the way. So I got him killed, after all. That's good."

Sonny shucked his knapsack from his shoulder to a table, and rummaged through the open top. "What made you so sure I did it?"

"It has your trademark all over it in blood."

Sonny pulled the videocassette that had come from Stead's camera out of his knapsack and held it up. "And my face is all over this. That TV man had it. I couldn't let him get away with it." He dropped the cassette on the table.

"You've managed to throw our planning out by almost a day. I've got forty men out there, and fifty more back at the mountain and I can't keep them waiting! We can make up the time if we work through the night. Starting now."

THE DRIVE to Zoreb Mountain over a rutted road led past fields and through a forest until limestone bluffs towered overhead, eighty feet of sheer vertical straight up to sky.

The valley was completely dark. While sunset endured beyond the mountains, here it was already night. The convoy from the Arkansas farmhouse came to a stop where the road ended, at a rock wall studded precariously with crooked pines until its ascent became too steep. The vehicles made themselves known by parking lights, and men with flashlights emerged from a dark cleft in the rock, greeting the new arrivals.

Friend or foe, there was no one within a radius of fifteen miles to hear them, but something about the primeval solitude of the forest and the rock made the men speak in hushed tones when they greeted one another. Quickly, one man waved the blue van to back into the opening in the limestone wall. Ronald Doule walked forward, his son and Keith Rotsky one step behind, and the rest of the men following. They disappeared into the shadowy cleft of Zoreb Mountain.

Brilliant overhead lights came on. The interior of the cave had been outfitted with a cement floor and gasoline storage tanks. At the farthest end, almost a hundred feet from the narrow opening, two metal doors opened onto an enormous elevator.

A battery-powered dolly whined and slipped in behind the van. The forklift rose, its tines moved forward under the crate containing the casket of stolen plutonium. The tines retracted, the fork lowered. Men moved in with hammers and crowbars, removed the wooden struts, until the yellow cylinder stood alone. Everything was carefully recorded on video by the cameraman. The dolly's motor whined again. The driver backed a half circle to turn it around, and headed for the elevator with his lethal cargo.

Zoreb Mountain had once been owned by a rich man, who converted the magnificent limestone caverns into a comfortable, two-story luxury—although windowless— home. It began as a bomb shelter just before the John Kennedy assassination, but by the time it was completed ten years later, the atom bomb scares were over. Since it no longer impressed the rich man's friends, he had had no further use for it.

Agents of the Aryan Nation used a million dollars in stolen bank funds to purchase the entire compound, which included the farmhouse at the front of the property. Later the rich man was killed, and knowledge of the cave's existence pretty much disappeared.

Behind the habitable parts, limestone caverns went on, seemingly forever. Forests of stalagmites were joined by galleries of rock, that led to cathedrals of ancient limestone leached and melted by the weight of aeons. Room for hundreds—even thousands of people. An entire army, their wives, children and slaves.

When the Aryan Nation had bought the land, it stockpiled food, weapons, gasoline and ammunition, waiting for doomsday, the overthrow of the federal government and the racial Armageddon that never quite seemed to come. But the organization had progressed since Ronald Doule, Sr., took over the leadership. Now they had a plan for instant retribution—unless the government gave in to their complete demands.

David Young, the missing scientist, had spent almost two weeks inside the mountain without having any idea where he was. He knew he was underground, because the place where he worked was a cave as big as a college gymnasium, where immense stalactites extended from the ceiling. A large concrete pad had been poured to smooth out the floor, and arc lights strung overhead illuminated the electronic equipment, tools and workbenches.

When the scientist wanted to sleep, the guards led him to another level in a large elevator. He heard the motor and felt the vibrations in the stainless steel cage, but he could not begin to estimate the speed of the elevator, or the vertical distance it traveled. It was only by the pull of gravity on his stomach that he knew he was going up.

When the cage stopped, a heavy door opened onto a sterile white corridor, as if he were emerging from a vast subterranean basement underneath a modern office building. A windowless room with a cot and a locked door was all he had to himself. Even his meals he took in the work area.

He didn't know if he was still in New Mexico or somewhere else. He didn't know what day it was, or even if it was day or night. Clocks and watches had been refused.

He knew who his captors were, though—at least by sight. Americans with bushy beards, camouflage fatigues and shotguns. Half a dozen men guarded him at all times, changing three times a day. Assuming they worked eight-hour shifts, it gave him a crude means to mark off time. Thirty-one shifts meant he'd been a prisoner more than ten days—not counting whatever time he had endured drugged into unconsciousness after being seized from the parking lot of the Los Alamos Federal Research Center.

Somewhere along the way he'd lost his glasses as well. His captors had replaced them with a pair of nonprescription reading glasses that gave him headaches. For some odd reason, they'd also pulled two of his teeth. His tongue moved reflexively to the right side of his mouth, exploring the healing gums where an upper and a lower molar had been extracted. They'd put him under with some gas one day, and when he regained consciousness in the cave, the teeth were gone.

Despite his insistent inquiries, no one answered his questions. Indeed, with one exception, no one spoke to him at all. The exception was a tall, barrel-chested man with black hair and a thick black beard. He was the one who had ordered him to build the nuclear bomb or die.

They had prepared a lab of sorts for him with an uncanny number of the correct materials—but after all, the information on how to build a nuclear bomb could be found in public libraries. And so he had worked feverishly until exhausted, sleeping little before working to the point of exhaustion again.

Building such a bomb was easy for someone as knowledgeable as Dr. Young, so easy he was surprised when people still refused to believe countries such as Israel, South Africa and Pakistan had nuclear arsenals. The physics involved was elementary by now.

Materials that he lacked, they easily and quickly procured. Gradually he was able to do what they asked. The fruit of his labors lay on a workbench in front of him, assembled inside the five-foot-long brass shell casing of an obsolete artillery gun—the intricate workings of a thermonuclear bomb. It was crude and somewhat makeshift, but it was also enough to destroy a medium-sized city like Hiroshima twenty times over. If he had the final ingredient—plutonium.

Young gambled that his captors didn't have it and wouldn't be able to supply it. Supplies of the lethal radioactive material were closely guarded, not only in the United States, but internationally. He hoped he was playing for time by building the bomb, praying that the police would find him first.

However, there could be no more stalling. His captors were going to ask him what more he needed to finish, and finally he would have to tell them. A metal so diabolically lethal it had been named for the ancient Roman god of the underworld.

The red light over the elevator door suddenly went on, taking Dr. Young's attention from the deadly object in front of him. Around the edges of the concrete slab, his weary guards raised their rifles slightly and stood a little bit straighter.

The doors opened. Ronald Doule, Sr., stood in front of his men, the soldiers of the Aryan Nation. He left the elevator, striding pompously across the cavern floor. Sonny and the Field Marshal sauntered several steps behind.

"Dr. Young!"

Captive faced captor. Doule stopped at the edge of the concrete pad. He was smiling happily. "I have something especially for you."

Doule snapped his fingers over his right shoulder. The men in the elevator moved out, revealing the forklift. Dr. Young recognized immediately the yellow container on the forks with its radiation hazard markings.

His heart sank. When he spoke again, his mouth was dry and his voice trembled. His words came out as a frightened whisper, which only increased Doule's pleasure, and broadened the smirk on Sonny's face.

"What are you going to do with . . . it?"

His sentence choked off at the end. The question Young wanted to ask concerned his own future, but he dared not. He had good reason to fear the answer. They had told him that when the bomb was finished, he would be released. He knew they were lying.

"What are we going to do with it!" the bearded patriarch crowed. "Hold America to ransom. Release all the Posse Comitatus and Aryan Nation prisoners in federal prisons. And give us an autonomous state in the Pacific Northwest where we can build a racially pure society."

Sonny moved out from behind his father, and there was a glazed look in his eyes. "Welcome, Dr. Young, to the second American revolution."

## 8

In Los Angeles, bevies of beautiful women strolled languidly through the luxurious rooms of a Bel-Air mansion, talking constantly, laughing too loudly, their eyes surreptitiously searching for this producer, that director, a movie star, someone or anyone whose casting couch might make a career.

It was the film biz.

It made him want to puke, especially because he'd been oversensitized since his one exposure.

Liam O'Toole, six-two, red hair, with the crusty lived-in face of an ex-sergeant, Vietnam veteran and sometime mercenary with a team of commandos known as the SOBs, was the wallflower of the party. He stayed in shadow, partly obscured by draperies at one side of a glass wall. On the other side, an immense kidney-shaped swimming pool, brilliant with light, stared into the starry night sky like a great aquamarine eyeball.

Liam O'Toole was also a writer—a poet, to be exact. His first collection, *Maggot Picnic*, which he had published himself, was a cult classic among certain species of bohemian punks. It was not what he had intended. What, after all, did punks know about the terror of war, the horror of death? From a youthful career as an IRA bomber to a noncom tour of duty in Nam, to numerous episodes on assignment with Nile Barrabas, O'Toole had seen it all.

Too much, in fact.

Yet looking at the yammering buxom babes come and go, speaking of Michelangelo or whoever it was who was getting laid lately, O'Toole knew he preferred the risk and tension of a do-or-die battle than the vapid mindlessness of Hollywood and Beverly Hills.

As far as Liam O'Toole was concerned, Los Angeles was the flake capital of the world. All talk, no action. Initially, the Irish American had been lured to the West Coast by talk of a lucrative offer for the film rights for a recent collection of poems, *Bullet Brain*. When he arrived a week earlier, he realized that was exactly what it was—all talk.

He'd been in and out of agents' offices, movie studios and production houses. The week was a blur of revolving doors. Everyone said the same thing—yeah, yeah, great book, terrific poetry, gonna be a hit, make ya a millionaire, see ya later.

Somehow in the course of things, he'd ended up with an invite to the Bel-Air party. The mansion was staggering in its opulence. Food and liquor was copious. Everyone had suntans. And so far, Liam O'Toole had scored zilch three times with the ladies.

No matter what he used for a come-on line, the conversation always ended up the same.

She asked, "What do you do?"

He said, "I'm a writer."

With each woman in turn, heavily mascaraed eyes glazed over. The first one suddenly became vague, pretended he was invisible and drifted off, like cigarette smoke vanishing into air.

The second one had been whisked away by a thin young man in a tuxedo with a pink bow tie, who kept sniffling, wiping his nose with his index finger and jerking his head toward the rest room in the foyer.

The third woman, a gorgeous well-developed blonde with a six-inch waist, almost gave him a chance. He told her he was the author of *Maggot Picnic*.

"Oh," she said, with apparent interest. Then she asked him, "Did you ever hear the story about the unsuccessful starlet?"

O'Toole shook his head, slightly mystified.

"She only slept with writers." The lady winked. Then she, too, was gone.

Three strikes you're out, O'Toole muttered to himself. Depressed and rejected, he cadged a triple Scotch at the bar, and stood in the corner all by himself, scowling at the beautiful, happy people who laughed just a little too loudly.

"The American way of life," he muttered to himself. "This is what I fight for?"

But he already knew the answer. He fought for himself. He fought because he had something inside him, a kind of rage that only a bottle of booze or the chatter of an auto-rifle eased. It was an addiction to the front line, the need for a fix of risk and danger. It was the job, the do-or-die missions that meant wiping out the kind of diabolical scum that bred misery in the lives of humankind. For Liam O'Toole, killing them made life worth living.

The only way he was able to express his profound feelings was in his epic poetry. But he knew it was wasted on Hollywood.

"I beg your pardon?"

The Irishman heard a light female voice at his side and turned to look.

She was gorgeous, tall and slender, with long red hair that curled luxuriantly down her bare shoulders. She wore a sleeveless green dress, her eyes were blue. Somehow, Liam O'Toole knew he had met her somewhere before.

"Just uh, talking to myself," he stammered. Then he snapped his fingers at the realization of whom he was talking to. "Miss February!"

She smiled slowly and slyly, and sipped champagne from her stem glass.

"Just call me Jezebel. Here's to you, Hunk. The most interesting man at this party."

She raised her glass toward his, while her eyes swept up and down his body, lingering slightly below the belt. Scotch clinked against champagne.

O'Toole indeed remembered, and it was more than Miss February. The redheaded Jezebel had been the cause of a flourish of headlines in the daily papers for her illicit affair with a famous born-again television evangelist. The evangelist had been tarred and feathered by the media, as well as his flock. Jezebel had gone on to a modeling career, particularly successful at modeling her naked body in the pages of indiscreet magazines.

She leaned against him, pushing her pelvis against his leg. O'Toole stiffened. Her voluptuous breasts rubbed against his biceps.

"A big rough-looking guy like you," she pouted. "It's been hell ever since I left my little house in Babylon, Long Island." She pronounced the *g* in *Long*, the true sign of a native.

O'Toole stretched his neck and pulled at the stiff collar of his dress shirt. Suddenly he felt hot and short of breath. Ball four, he could walk. He decided to make his move.

"Er, whaddya say we, uh—" He shrugged casually. "Find a place where we can, uh, be alone?"

"I'd love to!" Jezebel gushed. "You're the only *real* man I've met since I came to Hollywood."

Her tiny tongue darted across her crimson lips. She was breathing deep and fast. Her hard nipples pressed through her clothes like buttons. She raised herself on the toes of her high heels, leaned forward and kissed him lightly on the lips.

O'Toole breathed deeply the delightful scent of woman, his excitement mounting. Jezebel touched his chin with the red long nail of her index finger. Slowly, gently, she drew it under his chin, down his neck, over his chest, lingeringly slightly at his navel and dropping lower. Delicious shivers rippled up and down the merc's spinal cord. She kissed him again, this time just under the ear.

"Let's go upstairs," she whispered.

"My pleasure," O'Toole replied and followed her slow hip-swaying walk to the grand circular staircase that ascended from the ground-floor living room like a giant Slinky toy.

Neither of them noticed the commotion at the front door as they floated upstairs.

Walker "the Fixer" Jessup had flown in from Salt Lake City that afternoon and had spent the next five hours tracking down the elusive Irishman who served as Barrabas's second in command. Finally—on a tip from an executive assistant at the office of a producer, whom he had found after advice from the wife of an agent, whom he had tracked down after speaking to the desk clerk at the hotel where O'Toole was staying—the Fixer had arrived by limousine at the gates of the Bel-Air mansion.

It cost him four hundred dollars to pay off the gate-keeper, money that the tightfisted Texan begrudged mightily. He figured it might cost him another six to change the butler's attitude.

"I'm sorry, sir. You must present your invitation," the stiff-lipped Brit stated flatly, his nose at a forty-five-degree angle to the rest of the universe, and his eyes fixed on a spot two inches above Jessup's head.

It was precisely at that moment that the Texan saw an unmistakable head of red hair bob through the densely packed crowd of partygoers, and move up the staircase. The Irishman's hand fell to Jezebel's buttocks as they ascended together.

Jessup gasped, half from success in tracking down the Irishman, and half in appreciation of O'Toole's apparent success and his own rush of desire. And he had thought that food was all! Hurriedly he reached inside his jacket and plucked his wallet from the breast pocket.

"How much?" he asked. He slipped several hundred-dollar notes from the billfold. One at a time, he snapped the crisp paper money from one hand to the other.

The butler's eyes lowered, and his nose twitched. The servant looked quickly left and right. A hand reached out and clutched the money like the talon of a bird of prey seizing dinner.

"Enjoy yourself, sir." The man's face resumed its haughty expression, and he stood aside.

"I'll try," muttered the Fixer.

O'Toole had disappeared.

Walker Jessup headed for the stairs.

Liam and Jezebel easily found an empty bedroom in the farthest wing of the spacious mansion. Within seconds, they had stripped naked, clutching and grabbing at each other's bodies with a wild, unruly passion.

They fell onto the bed, rolling over and over, first one on top then the other, until they slid off the edge onto the carpet. Consumed by passion as they were, the fall stopped neither of them. Finally O'Toole stood, then sat on the bed, pulling Jezebel to him. Her red hair was wild, and her lipstick had been smeared across both their faces.

The Irishman hoisted the slender woman to his lap with her legs on either side of him.

"No, not like this," she cried between the deep sobbing breaths that racked her body. She whispered into his ear. O'Toole's eyes widened.

"What!" he exclaimed.

Jezebel pulled herself out of his lap and pushed past him, crawling across the bed on her hands and knees. With her voluptuous rear end held high, she turned her head back to look at O'Toole. "Take me," she cried on the verge of desperation. "Take me like a bitch in heat!"

In the second-floor hallway, Walker Jessup walked quietly along the carpet, and cursed the closed doors that led to bedrooms. He closed his eyes, crossed his fingers, opened his eyes and started his selection process.

"Eeny, meeny, miny mo . . ."

It was the second door on the right. He opened it. The dark writhing shapes on the bed were vividly silhouetted by the bright outdoor spotlights that illuminated the exterior of the house and spilled in the windows. Suddenly the couple stopped their wild gyrations.

"Get the hell out!" a man shouted furiously. It wasn't O'Toole. "Goddamn pervert!"

Jessup retreated, quickly slamming the door behind him. Just as he expected. The bedrooms were in use.

He braced himself and went on to the next.

Seven bedrooms later he counted up the toll. Three couples had screamed at him to get out. Four had invited him to join in, but at least two of them had involved the same sex.

Statistically normal for a flaky town like L.A.

One more door to go. Then it was up another flight to the servants' quarters.

He reached out to turn the handle when he heard noise within. He put his ear to the door. It sounded like a dog barking, and a furious struggle.

He reached inside his jacket and ripped his gun from the shoulder holster. His left hand hit the door handle and turned it. He kicked. The door swung open and slammed furiously against the inside wall.

"Hold it!" The Fixer crouched with arms extended and a two-handed grip on his pistol. He scanned the room with it, squeezing the trigger to within a hair of firing. He stopped at the strange configuration on the bed, perfectly silhouetted by light streaming through the curtains on the other side of the room.

Walker stepped back, his left hand falling from the gun and reaching blindly behind him to feel the wall. His fingers brushed the light switch. He flicked it on.

O'Toole and Jezebel were revealed to be inseparable. The Irishman was stunned at the sight of the massive Texan.

"Ohhh, don't stop now!" Jezebel moaned.

The Fixer smiled an uneasy, tinny smile, shuffled nervously and backed up. He snapped the lights out, put the gun back in its holster and stood in the doorway, arms akimbo.

"Five minutes, O'Toole," he said firmly. "I have an airplane to take us to Miami. Five minutes or else!"

"Oh yeah!" Liam wasn't fazed a bit. "Or else what?" he challenged.

"Or else I join you."

It was all that O'Toole needed to be persuaded.

Jessup stepped back, tapping his watch. "Five, Liam. Five minutes."

He closed the door quietly and slunk away.

THE SHOW WENT ON at Zoreb Mountain. It was like a Crazy Eddie commercial, the kind where the local guy who owns the used car lot or the discount stereo store makes a zany attempt at the big sell on midnight TV. But this was for real. Dr. David Young found it difficult to mask his horror at the macabre spectacle.

A man wearing a black cowl over his head stood under the glare of bright spotlights while another man video-taped him, and several dozen Posse men looked on. Behind him, a fake wall had been built to hide the cave, decorated with three huge letters, ZOG. A red circle had been painted around them, and a red diagonal line across the middle of it.

Young stood off to the side, still in his white lab coat. They allowed him to wander as freely as the thirty-foot chain yoked to his foot allowed. Yet still, the scientist was aware of the guarded looks that Posse men threw in his direction from time to time. They didn't miss a thing. Not even the troubled look on his face.

The man in the cowl was making a speech for the benefit of the camera. Young supposed he meant to sound Hitlerian with his loud strident tones and harshly barked words.

In reality, the guy sounded dumb. And extremely dangerous.

"We demand the release of all Aryan Nation prisoners in federal and state prisons!" The man in the cowl waved a clenched fist at the camera. "We demand the repeal of the sixteenth amendment to the Constitution. We demand the abolition of paper money and its replacement with gold and silver coins! We demand—"

It was the oddest mixture of racism and religion that Young had ever heard.

"We who are God's Chosen People, the ones who will follow the coming of the Messiah, and be the foot soldiers in the last battle of the great race war called Armageddon. The white people of America, that's who! Spawned by the union of angels with human women, we have been chosen to carry God's word, to undertake a mission to keep the white race pure! Free from contamination by Jews, who are the offspring of Satan. Free from the degeneracy of the negro race, mud people fit only for slavery! Free from the oppressive rule of the ZOG, the Zionist Occupation Government in Washington!''

The cameraman moved in for a close-up.

''We demand the creation of a racially pure nation, comprising the present territory of the states of Oregon and Washington. Should the Zionist Occupation Government fail to enter into immediate negotiations—''

Young heard a voice, barely a whisper, just behind him. ''Like what you're hearing?'' it asked in silken tones.

He turned and looked into the face of Sonny Doule. The young sovereign smiled benignly. Like a cat about to eat a budgie. It was at that precise moment that Dr. Young realized with certainty that they were going to kill him when he was finished loading the plutonium into the bomb.

''You're insane,'' Young hissed impulsively. ''I mean—'' he began to modify what he'd started to say, ''what do you plan on doing with this bomb!''

Sonny's blue eyes glittered coldly in the bright wash of lights. ''Come now, doctor. Don't pretend innocence for building it. You know bloody well how it's going to be used.''

''You said I'd be released after it was built!''

''Released!'' Sonny laughed. ''Well, that's one way to put it.''

''What are you doing with it?'' the kidnapped scientist demanded again.

''Tomorrow we'll seize a television station in Denver and broadcast this videotape to everyone in America. Get the truth out instead of all the lies we're told by the Jews who run New York and Washington.''

"But these demands are crazy. They'll never give your organization Oregon and Washington State.''

"Sure they will," Sonny replied confidently. "Or else we'll nuke a city where the maximum number of Jews and Negroes can be killed. Probably New York.''

The young sovereign gave the scientist a friendly slap on the back. "Maybe you'll be able to see the results of all your hard work in a few days," he said merrily.

"Cut!" a loud voice shouted. The big overhead TV spots were suddenly turned off, and the cavern was left with the cold white light from the fluorescent fixtures suspended over the lab area.

The speaker on the adjacent set pulled the cowl off his head. It was Ronald Doule, Sr. He threw the black mask to one of his men and sauntered over to Sonny and the scientist, stuffing a wad of chewing tobacco in his mouth.

"You got him ready yet?" Doule asked his son, chewing slowly on the tobacco.

"You can't be serious!" Young proclaimed, looking from the older man to the younger.

"Damn right we're serious. Never been more serious than now.''

"I refuse to arm the bomb. I don't care what you do to me.''

"Well, that gives us a problem," he said lazily, using his tongue to move the great mass of tobacco from one side of his mouth to the other.

Sonny pushed the scientist toward the lab, where the bomb lay on a table, showing a complex array of wires and circuits in the brass casing of the ancient artillery shell. Two men carried video equipment from the set used by

Doule. Others hustled to dismantle and move the spotlights.

"You're going to be in pictures!" Sonny taunted, grabbing Young by the sleeve of his lab coat and throwing him against the workbench.

Casually, Doule, Sr., spit a great gob of half-chewed tobacco onto the cement floor and pulled his .45 from his belt. He slammed the barrel into the scientist's forehead and held it there.

"This is the next scene, Dr. Young—you loading the plutonium into the bomb. We're going to take a very detailed videotape of everything—just so's they believe us out there that we ain't kidding around. We really mean business."

Young swallowed.

"Now git your ass over there and start doing it!" Doule Sr., cocked the gun with his thumb. The scientist felt nauseated.

He looked at the weapon of massive destruction that he had built and saw himself as an instrument of death, possibly the death of millions of Americans. And as much as he loved life, Dr. Young knew that if he allowed that to happen, his own survival would be worth nothing—to him or to anyone else.

His throat was dry, and he blanched, swallowing nervously. He nodded.

"Okay." The word came out barely a whisper. It was too late to say no. The police were not going to find him. And it occurred to the eminent nuclear physicist that now there was only one way out, and it was entirely up to him.

**9**

The Miami street looked naked, bathed in brilliant white sunlight, empty except for trash, burned-out cars and shopping centers whose signs creaked lazily in the slow humidity.

Miami baked. No one was outside. Riding low and easy, a turquoise '59 Cadillac eased to the curb and stopped. Three men got out. Alex "the Greek" Nanos, Claude Hayes and Billy Two. All were associates of Nile Barrabas. This time, though, the job was free-lance. In fact, it was volunteer.

A day earlier, a six-year-old girl had caught a stray bullet in a shoot-out between crack dealers. This part of the city was known as Little Havana, and it was Miami Boys territory. When a rival gang of Jamaicans tried to move in for a piece of the narcotics action, the street had turned into a battle zone, and the little girl was an innocent casualty.

The three professional soldiers had returned to Miami after the raid in Amarillo for some sportfishing in the waters off the Florida Keys. Before they got out of their hotel, the story of Miami's crack wars unfolded on the news.

That part of the Cuban neighborhood was so dangerous that police refused to go there. Gang members were armed with everything from MAC-10s and Uzis to grenades and the occasional rocket launcher.

Fresh from the job at the Amarillo farmhouse, Nanos Hayes and Starfoot decided to teach the drug punks a lesson they'd never forget.

The Miami Boys operated from an abandoned motel on a wide stretch of road where shopping centers were distant islands far across oceans of cars.

On one side of the highway, another mall was about to be erected. Bulldozers stood idle in a city of ferroconcrete frames. Off the road on the other side, behind the motel there were streets of small and dilapidated frame houses, many of them abandoned and burned out. The mercs were parked a block northwest of the Miami Boys' headquarters.

Despite the heat, the men wore bulky olive drab fatigues over bulletproof vests, with web belts amply loaded with extra ammo. They looked quickly for signs of life, opened the trunk and scooped out their weapons—two Uzi submachine guns, three Berettas with silencers, and for Billy Two a double-barreled .00-gauge shotgun.

"The mincemeat meet-your-maker maker," Billy Two rhymed off, reaching for the shotgun. The Indian brandished the ugly snout-nosed weapon, handling it with obvious comfort. Nanos put a Beretta into his belt, and slipped an Uzi under his jacket, Hayes likewise. Each of the men threw several tear gas grenades in their pockets.

"Eleven-thirty." Nanos looked at his watch, and the other two checked theirs. "We move at 11:35 exactly."

The abandoned motel was L-shaped and two stories high, a faded fuchsia-trimmed affair against peeling white. The frame exterior and the extinct neon sign at the edge of the parking area were liberally spray-painted with slogans and Miami Boys' colors. Two shiny new Jeep Cherokees were parked in the broken drive in front of the ground floor.

A balcony ran around the upper level, and overlooked an enormous swimming pool, empty of water, more recently a city dump. At night, rats played among rotting mattresses and rusting appliances that had been thrown there. Billy Two knew. He had lain among them in the darkness when the mercs did their reconnaissance the night before.

There were always three guards, one at either end of the L, and one in the crook. The two closest to the street were only lookouts, however. What weapons they had were hidden under their clothes. The one in the center was a different story. He had a machine gun.

He was squat and wide, and bulged with massive muscles. The M-60 was suspended by a thick leather strap strung around his broad back. The chain of bullets looped out of one side, and was wrapped in circles around his shoulders.

The plate-glass windows and the doors to each unit had long been covered with plywood, and according to news reports, the plywood served to disguise plates of quarter-inch steel. Small slits appeared across them at regular intervals, providing peepholes for surveillance as well as a place to shoot from. The abandoned motel had been transformed into a virtual fortress.

In the center of one wing, the plywood had been torn from a doorway and replaced by steel. Again, there were small grilled slits for a guard inside to see out. But the mercs had scanned the building with infrared heat detectors, and by tracking the heat images they knew that the motel had been riddled with interior doorways leading from unit to unit, upper level to lower level. As Nanos commented dryly, it was like an ant farm inside.

"It's time," Claude Hayes said softly to the others.

With the calm efficiency of professionals, they salute
by grasping fists together and shaking once before pulling
apart. It was like a football huddle, but the men were grim
and tight, tense from their adrenaline high. They split up
Hayes in one direction, Nanos and Billy Two down an
other street at right angles to the one Hayes took.

Two minutes later, Billy Two and Alex Nanos parted
The massive Indian loped across the road toward the con
struction site.

The son of an Osage chief who had struck it rich with oi
wells on Indian property, Starfoot had long been dis
owned by his family. He had been accused of following the
white man's ways. In fact, it was quite the opposite. The
family immersed themselves in every luxury money could
buy, and ruthlessly sold off mineral rights on Indian land
to the highest bidder. The wilderness that had once been
entrusted to the tribe was being desecrated.

Billy Two had run away as a teenager to become a Ma
rine commando. He was an expert tracker and survivalist
And he'd been glad to join Barrabas, but he'd become
prone to being a little crazy at times. An assignment in
Russia had resulted in his imprisonment and psychiatric
torture behind the Iron Curtain. It was there, with liquid
sulfur burning through his veins, that he first met Hawk
Spirit.

The vision of the ancestral Osage warrior god had ap
peared during his worst moments of indescribably excru
ciating pain. Spectral or real, somehow Hawk Spirit had
guided him through the maelstrom of insanity that beck
oned the drug-ravaged merc.

Since his escape and the revenge he extracted on hi
wardens, Hawk Spirit appeared to him sporadically
sometimes in the form of an intuition, sometimes as the
gut feeling of instinct, sometimes with an absolute con

viction of what the future held or a vision of someone in trouble. And sometimes, Billy Two swore by the souls of his ancestors, Hawk Spirit made him invisible and invulnerable.

There were three big yellow bulldozers to choose from, so the Osage chose the newest. He climbed into the seat, slipping needle-nosed pliers and a screwdriver from his pocket. Working quickly and deftly, he removed a plate under the control panel and clipped two wires. When he joined them together, the engine roared to life.

He checked his watch. Three minutes to go.

He disengaged the clutch and put the gears in reverse to back up. He moved the bulldozer until it was directly opposite the motel, two hundred feet away. That was when he realized he was a sitting duck. A gunman barely had to aim to blast him out of his seat.

For a moment, Billy Two considered relying on Hawk Spirit to protect him. Lately, however, the warrior god had been notable by his absence. It was months since they had communicated. It occurred to Billy Two that Alex Nanos was right. Hawk Spirit was a figment of his gravid imagination, spawned by psychiatric treatment in a Russian hospital. If so, maybe after several years he was getting better. That was good. But Billy Two missed his spirit guide and friend.

He had a minute left. His hand moved to the control for the big blade. He raised it until it was locked just above the dozer's engine, blocking his view but providing a bulletproof shield of half-inch steel. There was a narrow crack he could peer through between the hood and the bottom of the blade.

He checked his watch again. It was time to go.

Nanos stood flat against the back of the motel. There was a narrow covered driveway running between the first motel unit and the burned-out office. The Miami Boy guard paced twenty feet away, his sneakers scuffing at the cracked pavement.

Claude was in the same position behind the other wing. The two men carefully watched the second hands on their watches as the last thirty seconds ran out.

Cradling his Uzi with his elbow, Nanos pulled a small cigarette from his jacket pocket and, without putting it in his mouth, lit it. The acrid odor of marijuana quickly filled the air. Alex snatched it from his mouth and waved his hand. A cloud of smoke billowed along the wall of the motel. The Greek waited.

A few seconds later, the lookout smelled it. His nose twitched and he sniffed at the air, his curiosity piqued by the familiar smell. He looked around the corner and saw no one.

Alex dropped the joint, and once again flattened himself against the wall. He heard the guard approach the corner, the soft tread of his sneakers on the crumbling driveway, the movement of his body in clothes. Nanos let the Uzi hang and dug the Beretta from his belt.

The lookout walked into the open, still sniffing his way to the source of the joint. Startled, he saw the Greek. His eyes widened as he realized what was happening. Alex fired.

The silenced gun coughed. A single red eye opened, perfectly centered between the lookout's eyes. The back of his head exploded in a spray of blood, bone and brain. His body folded up noiselessly.

Alex stood and listened carefully at the humid breeze. Somewhere not far away he heard an engine roar like a great beast. It was growing louder as the beast approached. He nodded to himself, moved forward and peered around the next corner.

At the center of the two wings, the machine gunner noticed the lookout was gone. He spoke into a hand-held radio, telling the guard at the other end. Then he walked toward the corner that hid Nanos.

The other guard at the far end of the motel watched his boss saunter away to investigate the lookout's disappearance. Hayes stepped forward. The black warrior's massive hand came down on top of the guard's head. The gang member saw the blade of a long knife glint in the brilliant Florida sunlight. It swooped down and blood spurted into his frame of vision.

Hayes jerked the man's head back, snapping the vertebrae and throwing the body down. He was done. He spun around the corner.

The machine gunner, now the only surviving guard, reached the end of the row of units, his attention caught by the bulldozer leaving the entrance to the construction sight across the street. Without warning, Alex Nanos flew around the corner.

The Beretta coughed again, twice, and the man was flung aside, his face destroyed by the impact of the bullets. The M-60 landed across his chest.

Bullets pounded into the corner of the motel, eating their way across the wood toward Nanos. He flung himself back behind the corner, feeling a passing round kick the heel of his shoe. He rolled, pulling his feet in. Standing quickly, he reached for the machine gun lying across the dead man's body.

Someone inside the motel had clued in to the attack. The firefight was starting to heat up.

The bulldozer veered sharply off the road onto the cracked and broken driveway that ran into the parking lot.

Along the front of the motel, the small slits cut into the plywood across the windows bristled with the bellicose snouts of MAC-10s, assorted calibers of rifles and semi-automatic pistols. The parking area exploded with a volley of gunfire. A hail of bullets pinged into the bulldozer and ricocheted violently in all directions. Chunks of rubber were torn from the giant treads.

But the beast came on. Billy Two crouched in the seat, eyeing the front of the motel through a narrow crack between the blade and the hood over the engine. His huge hands gripping the stick gears, he felt the machine vibrating from bullet shivers running through the metal frame. A steady high-pitched ringing emanated from the thick steel blade.

He lined the dozer up for the weakest part of the Miami Boys' fortress—between the plate-glass windows of two units. The thick blade punched through the walls as if they were cardboard. The steel plates over the windows popped, bowling over the gang members who had taken cover behind them. The wall between the two units splintered and folded like an accordion of crushed two-by-fours.

In one unit, women screamed. The Miami Boys' gang members fled to other units through the openings that honeycombed the interior walls.

Alex Nanos appeared in the open gap behind the bulldozer. He stood like an intrepid explorer, the dead guard's machine gun firmly in hand. Gripping the twenty-five-pound M-60 tightly, his muscular arms were knotted with thick veins. He swung the barrel of the M-60, the leather strap digging into his neck, and pulled the trigger.

The M-60 chomped through the chain link, spewing empty shells from the side. Bullets ripped savagely across the walls, chewing away plaster and wallboard, chasing the last of the gang members into the adjacent unit, leaving several machine-gunned corpses in their wake. A cloud of dust and debris hung in the air.

Billy Two braked a little and turned the bulldozer sharply to the left. The giant blade dug into wall, bending it like plastic until it snapped in two. The exterior wall on one side began to peel away like a sardine can, while overhead, the ceiling under the second story began to sway dangerously.

The bulldozer swept forward, pushing a huge pile of rubble ahead of it. The gang members had fled deeper into the motel. Billy Two spun the throttle on full again and dozed forward. The next wall fell over like a bookshelf crashing down, amid the sound of shattering glass.

Golden light flickered across the skin of the bulldozer and the ceiling. The steel window had popped on the far wall, and sunlight streamed in.

Bullets spattered into the smashed walls of the motel from gang members in units in the other wing, pinging wildly against the side of the dozer and ripping through one of the Jeeps parked out front. But the Miami Boys were holed up in a dead end, safe for the time being behind their barricades of steel but with no place to run to and no place to hide.

The Osage heard Claude Hayes shout through the deafening noise of the bulldozer, the guns and destruction. He pulled the throttle down and jumped to cover behind the dozer.

Hungry tongues of fire curled up the wall in front of him. What was left of the room was filled with a disarray of smashed glass bottles that had crashed from tables. Flames spread in great gulps across flammable liquids that spilled from the broken vessels.

Hayes ran across the heaps of rubble, dodging bullets and swerving to avoid the sharp splinters of shattered beams skewed through the debris. He leaped behind the dozer and shouted at Billy Two. "It's a crack factory, this whole place is going to blow!"

Nanos crouched behind a piece of broken wall on the other side of the hole made by the bulldozer's initial entrance. He motioned for Hayes and Billy Two to wait.

Cradling the M-60 carefully and adjusting the links around his neck, he jumped into the open, firing from the hip. He waded across the sidewalk outside the unit, maintaining his barrage, and crouched behind one of the Jeep Cherokees. Bullets chewed a zigzag line across the facade of the other wing, interrupting for a moment the hail of lead from the cornered gang.

Billy Two abandoned the bulldozer. Crouching to keep down, he and Claude Hayes ran through the opening smashed into the side of the motel until they were at Nanos's side behind the Jeep. The storm of autofire resumed anew, and the vehicle shuddered from the impact of hundreds of MAC-10 9 mm bullets.

Black smoke was pouring from the gaping wound in the side of the building. Behind it a wall of flame flickered angrily.

"We gotta go!" Hayes shouted to the Greek. "If that's a drug factory in there, it's full of ether and kerosene. It'll blow the moment the flames get to it."

Alex jerked his head toward the corner of the hotel. Hayes and Billy Two nodded. To give them cover, the Greek spun into the open, the machine gun blasting. Hayes and Billy Two sped across the distance of the remaining two units and ducked behind the corner.

"Get the car!" the black SOB told Billy Two. The Osage handed Hayes his double-barreled shotgun and bounded down the street, his long legs making incredible leaping strides.

Hayes swung around the corner, shouting at Nanos to run. Through the smoke and dust, he spotted movement in the ruins of the motel. One of the Miami Boys had somehow survived the initial attack and was fleeing through the flames. He had a weapon, and he was aiming to shoot Nanos in the back.

Hayes raised the shotgun and squeezed the trigger. The brutal weapon spit its flesh-chewing rounds, impacting in the punk's gut and slicing his torso in two.

Nanos kept the M-60 at his hip and turned around when Hayes opened up. He kept firing the machine gun and ran backward toward Hayes. By the time the two men were abreast, dirty black smoke from the motel billowed across the parking lot, providing a screen. Both men turned and ran across the pothole-studded gravel yard behind the motel.

The turquoise Cadillac screeched around the corner at the end of the street, its whitewalls throwing out blue smoke. Nanos and Hayes reached it just as the tanks of ether blew. A sound like the crack of thunder and a shock wave washed over them. A massive gas fireball roiled above the motel, and flames engulfed the building, sweeping through it unit by unit in rapid procession.

The Miami Boys who survived the commando assault were instantly incinerated.

Billy Two slammed the brakes and the '59 Caddy lurched to a halt. Nanos jumped into the front seat, Hayes the back. The Indian crushed the gas pedal to the floor, and the Caddy zoomed away up the road. Sirens, heralding the approach of police cars from all directions, quickly grew distant behind them.

"Hell!" the Greek exclaimed. "I could feel that heat wave go right over me when that motel blew!" He was panting for breath, still clutching the M-60, his olive skin drenched in sweat and dirt. He turned to look at Hayes in the back seat.

"I'd sure hate to be in those suckers' place," he summed up his feelings on the matter.

"At least they won't be shooting any more six-year-old girls and getting off scot-free for it," Claude Hayes intoned solemnly.

"SOBs rush in where police fear to tread," added Alex, "but I must admit I nearly bought it there a couple of times. Maybe what everybody needs is a little free-lance work every now and then, and we can be the scourge of crack dealers everywhere. Just to help clean up things a bit—the Drug Enforcement Administration could use a little of our secret manpower."

Claude Hayes looked across the seat at the Greek. "Alex, that's not a bad idea. But let's face it, being vigilantes means treading a pretty thin line. Between being a hero and being a criminal."

"Humph!" Billy Two grunted. "First we're heroes. Then we're arrested. Then we're locked up and white man throws away key. Meanwhile, no room in jails for drug dealers. This is white man's way."

Hayes and Nanos smiled.

"My man, you sure got it figured out!" Nanos told Billy Two with a wink at Hayes.

Starfoot sailed down Everglades Boulevard, and soon the old Cadillac was crossing the causeway to Miami Beach. By the time the three men reached their hotel, the elimination of the Miami Boys' crack house was all over the radio, reported as a violent and bloody encounter between rival gangs that led to an explosion in a cocaine laboratory. Police and firemen were searching the ruins. So far, there were no survivors.

Parking in the underground garage, the three men quickly secreted their weapons in the trunk and headed for the stairs to the main lobby.

The entire venture had lasted barely an hour, and less than ten minutes of it had been combat. But the battle high had left, and with it gone, a certain fatigue fell over them. It was always the same—whether the battle lasted a week or a couple of minutes. Adrenaline kept a soldier alert, and fueled the rage for fighting, but the body's resources were taxed enormously.

They mounted the steps to the hotel's cathedral lobby in silence. The Belle Fontaine was one of Miami Beach's older hotels, built in 1960 with a certain plastic elegance. They headed across the sea of baby-blue carpeting toward the bank of elevators on the other side of the front entrance. Noticing the stares of passing tourists, the three men realized they looked like hell. Their faces and arms were blackened with dirt and smoke, and their fatigues had been ripped and soiled.

"I could sure use a sauna and a little, you know, poontang!" Nanos winked, stretching his muscular arms and shoulders to keep post-battle stiffness at bay. His eyes wandered to the three-story-high glass wall that fronted the hotel's outsize swimming pool and beyond, the Atlantic Ocean.

Dozens of luscious women lounged with great nonchalance there although they were nearly naked, glistening with oil and lotions under the frying light of the golden sun. Alex fought the impulse to dive in immediately. He was like a kid in a candy store.

"Nanos, since when can't you use a little poontang?" Claude Hayes muttered from the side of his mouth.

"I'm a healthy guy, I got hormones!" the Greek protested, turning to his buddy. "Besides, it's a great way to release tension."

Abruptly, Billy Two stopped in front of the two men. Nanos slammed into him facefirst and stumbled back.

"Forget poontang!" the Osage stated flatly. "Trouble comes."

"Oh shit!" Hayes groaned. "They followed us from the motel." He looked around the massive Indian, searching the lobby for the police. When he saw who was striding across the baby-blue carpet, he groaned again.

"Police?" Alex asked, rubbing his nose.

Hayes shook his head. "Worse."

"Miami Boys?"

The black man shook his head.

Before he could say anything further, the voice with its distinctive Texas drawl boomed across the hotel lobby. "Just the men I was looking for!"

Now it was Alex's turn to groan. He knew the voice. Walker Jessup, a.k.a. the Fixer. He stepped out from behind Starfoot and saw the fat man charging toward them. Twenty feet behind him, just beyond the glass doors that led outside, Liam O'Toole paced slowly back and forth.

Nanos put his hands up as if he was warding off a vampire. "We promise. We won't do it again. We took a risk, I know. But it was a favor we were doing. For a six-year-old girl! I mean, the little girl's dead. That's why we did it for her. I mean, not for her, it was revenge, sort of. Not revenge. Sort of free-lance work, you know, to clean up the streets and make them decent for—"

Jessup stood in front of the three SOBs, staring with bewilderment at the Greek.

"Alex, since when have you been concerned about decency?" He turned to the others. "What's he talking about?"

Hayes couldn't resist a smile at Nanos's panic. "We just got involved in a little brawl with some crack dealers," he said in his slow laconic voice.

For the first time, Jessup noticed their dirty faces and tattered fatigues. His eyes widened slightly before he suppressed his surprise.

"Well whaddaya know," he said lazily, his eyes narrowing shrewdly. The surprise on his face was replaced by a devious smile. "All dressed up and no place to go. Have I got a proposal for you!"

With those words, he moved beside the three men and graciously beckoned them toward the hotel doors. Outside, Liam O'Toole turned around and spotted his three buddies. A smile split his face from ear to ear. He waved and shouted something that they didn't hear through the glass doors.

"Hawk Spirit say great white leader has big plans for terrible battle," Billy Two chanted solemnly, his brow furrowed and his eyes staring upward at some invisible spot on the ceiling.

Jessup snapped his fingers and looked up at the six-foot-seven-inch Indian. "Why Starfoot, you're a goddamn visionary!"

"Hawk Spirit commands," the Osage said in an even monotone. "I merely obey."

Sometimes Billy Two's communication with his ancient ancestor spirit had uncanny results. This time, however, Jessup was willing to swear on a Bible that a smile tugged at the corner of the Osage's lips.

"So what's up, Walker?" Hayes asked finally, characteristically straightforward. "The colonel got something for us to do?"

"As Alex put it, a little free-lance work," Jessup replied happily, looking at the Greek. "To make the streets safe from some of the most heinous scum that America has ever faced."

"Not bad," the Greek said and nodded. It was the kind of assignment he could get his teeth into. Then he remembered the sauna waiting for him upstairs, and the bevies of smooth-skinned women lounging around the pool. "Time for a shower?" he asked tentatively.

On the other side of the glass front doors, Liam O'Toole motioned with his thumb toward a limo waiting at the curb. Then he raised his arm and pointed impatiently at his watch.

"Car's waiting," Jessup drawled, again extending his hand in a gracious gesture to motion them ahead. Once more, his eyes swept over their torn and disheveled fatigues and sweaty faces.

"This war," he deadpanned, "is strictly come-as-you-are."

## 10

The next day began gently enough, a warm air mass moving gradually through the Midwest, pushed by cooler air blowing down off the Rockies. Where the two currents met, thunder and lightning erupted in extravagant storms. While in Utah the SOB mercenaries rendezvoused in driving rain, in northern Arkansas Ronald Doule, Sr., bade goodbye to his son under blue skies and warm sunlight.

By early morning a convoy had assembled in front of the Aryan Nation farmhouse with the practiced efficiency of a military movement. Forty men, dressed in battle fatigues and armed with a variety of semiautomatic and automatic weapons, piled into the backs of two half-ton, olive drab trucks.

A battered black Jeep idled in front of the house. Spiker and Chuka sat in the front seats. Nearby, Ronald Doule, Sr., and Sonny watched the men pull the flaps over the back of each truck. The trucks swung into line behind the Jeep. Guards paced back and forth around the convoy.

"This is it," Sonny said finally, turning to his father. "Hard to believe, ain't it? After two years of planning..."

"Two years?" The bearded patriarch shook his head. "A lifetime. This was my dream for you the moment you were born eighteen years ago, Sonny."

"Well, it's all gone like clockwork."

"Pretty much," Doule said, somewhat reluctantly. His eyes wandered over the bruises that still marked Sonny's face from the fight in Rock Springs. His son seemed edgy, almost reluctant to leave.

The leader of the Aryan Nation handed the young man a black box containing the videocassette of the "news conference" that had been taped inside Mount Zoreb. "The next stage of the plan depends entirely on you now," he told Sonny.

Sonny took the cassette and clutched it tightly, aware of an awesome responsibility. Still, he seemed reluctant to go.

"How long do you think it'll be before you get us back here?" Sonny asked finally.

"Once you seize the television station and broadcast our demands nationwide, the entire country will panic. They'll give us everything we want. We'll be together in a matter of days."

"Maybe even in our own country," Sonny said to show his optimism. His father had never discussed what would happen if the authorities stonewalled, or just said no and besieged the television station. Sonny himself had dismissed it as a possibility, only because it was the worst of alternatives. His father had never let him down before. He had no reason to expect that Doule, Sr., would now, either.

Somewhere a walkie-talkie speaker squawked, and a guard ran up to the two men.

"Our spotter at the valley door says a black Mercury is heading for the ranch."

"Let it through," Doule ordered him. "It's a man named Heiss. He's come all the way from Washington to see me." The big bearded man turned back to his son. "You see," he told Sonny. "Already we attract the attention of important people."

"I have to go, Father. It's a thirteen-hour drive. Then the action begins."

Father and son embraced quickly. Sonny leaped into the back of the Jeep and waved as it moved off. The two half-ton trucks rolled after it, picking up speed and hastening to their final destination.

NILE BARRABAS and Jake Larraby were ready and waiting at a mountain cabin north of Salt Lake City when Jessup finished his peripatetic crisscrossing of the continent in his chartered Jet.

After Jessup rounded up O'Toole, the three men in Miami and Lee Hatton in Boston, mechanical difficulties kept the mercs at Boston airport most of the night. By the time they arrived in Salt Lake City, it was dawn. Then they faced a sixty-mile drive to a remote ranch northwest of the city, a temporary hideout supplied through resources of Barrabas's old friend, Jake Larraby. Fortunately, Claymore Jeffries had arranged for an FBI car to be put at their disposal in Salt Lake City before he returned to Washington.

A driving rain still fell when the mercs left the car and ran across a yard into the small frame cabin where Barrabas and Larraby waited. Alex Nanos was the first one inside the house, running fast with a poncho over his head and shoulders. Water poured down off the folds of the canvas and ran onto the floor. The Greek peeked out from under it like a drowned rat.

Barrabas couldn't resist laughing at the obvious discomfort of the suave lady's man.

"Little rain?" he teased.

"We are not talking rain," Nanos said, pronouncing each word loudly and carefully. "We are talking deluge. We are talking Biblical proportions, y'know, like forty days and forty nights!" He waved his arms to emphasize his point, and the poncho tumbled onto the floor.

Suddenly Lee Hatton bounded in, then Billy Two, Claude Hayes and Liam O'Toole, laughing and barging against one another, pushing Nanos farther into the room. They all carried a duffel bag each, which they tossed into a pile. Suddenly the cabin seemed filled up.

It was rustic, the interior only half-finished, with beams and joists in the ceiling and walls still exposed, but comfortably furnished with overstuffed sofas. A small kitchen was visible through a doorway, and stairs led up to bedrooms. A fire burned in the massive stone fireplace on one side.

The mercs greeted their colonel warmly. It was a week since their last morning together, in Amarillo, Texas, a relatively short period of time between missions. Then Jessup walked in the door, and the space seemed to diminish. He was drenched to the bone, his gray wool suit plastered against his torso.

Lee Hatton fought to restrain a laugh. The Fixer looked like Humpty Dumpty, but far too miserable to make fun of.

Jessup looked miserable because he was. So far, the chartered Lear jet had run up a bill of slightly in excess of half a million dollars. It was going to make a dent in petty cash. Jessup glared at the high-spirited group, his lip rising in an unfriendly curl.

Nanos was pounding O'Toole on the shoulder, and the big Irishman swung around, putting his forearm up to block. "Miss February, was it!" Nanos taunted. "That little evangelical minister's bimbo. Is it true she takes it like a dog?"

A dreamy look passed over Liam's eyes, and he smiled smoothly. "She says she learned everything from the preacher."

Suddenly a gun fired in their midst, abruptly halting conversation. Jessup stood with his Walther P-38 smoking in one hand, pointed above his head.

"Hear me now and believe me later!" he roared over the sound of rain pounding on the roof.

In the slight pause that followed, a plump raindrop dripped through the newly made bullet hole in the roof, directly onto Jessup's head. He looked up. A second drop landed squarely between his eyes. He stepped forward out of the way and addressed the mercs once again.

"I am going to turn around, and get in that car in my soaking-wet clothes and drive back to Salt Lake City, where I will board the chartered jet for Washington, D.C. Jeffries wants me to meet with him there. He wants me to have a look at why the National Security Council got involved in pulling the FBI off this whole case.

"Now so far, that Lear has cost plenty, and I still don't have a client to bill for it. So whatever you guys do in the next day or so, I hope it puts this problem to bed once and for all. If you happen to see any bags of spare cash lying around, you might confiscate them in the name of your wages. Any matériel you need, make sure I know. Jeffries will supply. The colonel has the D.C. number."

Jessup raised one arm in a kind of salute. "Good luck, one and all."

With that, the fat man retreated into the pouring rain, which obscured his figure even before he reached the car.

Barrabas closed the door of the cabin, cutting off the spattering sound of the driving rain. In the sudden quiet, the mercs listened to the drum of rain on the roof, and the sizzle and crackle of logs in the fireplace.

"So what've you got for us, Colonel?" Hayes asked, standing by Billy Two.

Before Barrabas could reply there was a howl of delight from the kitchen.

"Wow!" Something had caught the Greek's attention. "Check this out, guys!"

Barrabas tilted his head toward the kitchen. "Let's join Alex."

The spectacle that amazed the Greek was spread across the floor of the cabin's half-finished kitchen. There were two open crates of grenades packed in straw like rare eggs, half a dozen M-16s with hundreds of spare mags. As well, there was a Vietnam war-vintage M-79 grenade launcher, or "thumper" as the grunts had called it. With the weapons the mercs had brought in their duffel bags, they were armed for a small war.

Jake Larraby gleefully demonstrated the last item in his arsenal to Alex Nanos. "Zippo the flamethrower," he named it affectionately, looking up when the other mercs piled into the room.

"Just a few things that've helped me out from time to time going after cattle rustlers," he told them all with a twinkle in his eye.

Barrabas introduced his old friend to the team. "Our target is a ranch compound in the hills north of here. It's isolated and fortified. But Jake here says he knows the back way in."

"When do we do it?" Lee Hatton demanded in a no-nonsense tone of voice.

"Rain's supposed to pass by in two or three hours," Jake told them. "I gotta get our transportation lined up. Might as well grab yourselves some shut-eye while you can."

"Hey Jake!" Hayes shouted boisterously. "What I wanna know is how you use a flamethrower against cattle rustlers. Or is that for the barbecue when you get the cows back?"

The mercs laughed, with Jake joining in.

"We call 'em cattle out this way," Larraby crowed. "Cows is what you eastern folks grow!"

As the laughter died, the cowboy hoisted the tanks of flammable liquids onto his back with a practiced movement.

"I've barbecued with it," he told them, holding the funnel-shaped torch in front of him as though it was a vacuum cleaner hose. "But I haven't tried cattle yet. No sir. Since I'm gettin' on in years, with a bad back, I get kind of tired chasing after rustlers all the time. Hell, the flame on this thing stretches out sixty feet before you can say 'pass the marshmallows.'"

He dropped the torch and began shucking off the tanks. "Not many rustlers can outrun a hot licking from my old friend Zippo the flamethrower."

By noon the weather had cleared, and the sun shone warm and golden over the deep blue dome of Utah sky. The mercenaries left the unfinished cabin in Barrabas's newly replaced red Bronco and Jake's old Jeep Cherokee. They took a secondary highway that led off Interstate 15, and soon were traveling through the desolate uninhabitable mountains along the edge of Great Salt Lake.

An hour after they left, the two vehicles turned onto a small undivided road that led into a narrow canyon, where red stone walls towered in sheer verticals above them. Suddenly the canyon opened into a wide valley. Pine trees climbed the slopes and forested the bottom, where a narrow river ran like a blue snake along the valley floor.

Water from the heavy rains had already evaporated under the rays of the fierce hot sun and dry warm breezes, but wildflowers had sprung up literally overnight, and tossed their colorful petals along the side of the road or in fields of a burned-out forest. The pristine valley was a hidden paradise in the dry inhospitable badlands that covered much of northern Utah.

The road led to the far end of the valley and around an old mountain that had been worn down by aeons of erosion like the stump of an old tooth. The sides and top were heavily forested with spindly pine trees, and the weathered log buildings of the Doule ranch were strung along a plateau like the walls of a citadel. A gravel road, barely a narrow yellow slash between two sides of the forest, wound its way back and forth up the side of the mountain. It was impossible to enter the valley or approach the ranch without being spotted.

"Long as we just travel on through, they won't think nothing of us," Jake told Billy Two from the wheel of his ancient Jeep. "We'll pull over on the other side of that there mountain. There's a foot trail that leads up from there."

"How long you figure it'll take us to climb it?" Lee Hatton asked from the back seat. Like Claude Hayes who sat beside her, and the other mercs riding behind them in Barrabas's 4x4, she wore camouflage greens and heavy black steel-toed boots.

"A good hour if we push it," Larraby told her. "Uphill all the way."

Twenty minutes later, Jake pulled over and stopped. He got out of his Jeep and walked to the Bronco, which Barrabas parked behind him. He leaned in the open window to talk.

"An old logging road leads in here about half a mile," he told the colonel. "The trail up the mountain leads off from there. I dunno how far we can get, what with that heavy rain and all. If we get bogged down we'll have to walk it."

With both vehicles in four-wheel drive, the mercs experienced bone-wrenching jolts and bounces as they negotiated fallen trees and muddy sloughs that cut the road in several places. Jake stopped again, backed his vehicle's tail end into the pine forest and turned around to face out. Barrabas did likewise. The mercs stepped from the vehicles, relieved to have finally arrived.

Barrabas checked his chronometer. It was almost two o'clock in the afternoon. The sun had passed its high point, but its rays burned hotter. Nature appeared glorious, with light breezes playing through the aromatic branches of the pines, and small songbirds warbling and fluttering from tree to tree.

Alex Nanos and Lee Hatton were divvying up weapons from the back of the Jeep. Barrabas grabbed the stock of an M-16. Then Lee handed him magazines, which he jammed into the deep pockets of his camou fatigue pants and web belt. Claude Hayes appropriated the thumper and packed a supply of grenades into his web belt. Once again Billy Two had his double-barreled shotgun. Liam O'Toole went for an M-16. It wasn't necessarily the finest automatic weapon, but it was familiar to him from his days in Nam. Jake took another M-16 with a powerful sniper scope. Lee and Alex stuck with the small, lightweight Uzis they had brought with them.

With an onerous climb ahead of them, the men and Lee stripped off their fatigue jackets to reveal dark green and black T-shirts. Their muscular arms glistened with sweat. Lee Hatton's small delicately boned body concealed beneath her feminine curves the wiry agility of a lethal expert in the martial arts.

Jake estimated the climb would take an hour. The mercs synchronized their watches. Claude Hayes and Liam O'Toole each climbed behind the wheel of one of the 4x4's.

Barrabas held up a flare and then tucked it into his belt.

"Wait forty minutes here, then drive up the main road to the ranch house," he told them. "If you see grape before then, don't wait. Come right away and get us." The flare would expel a plume of highly visible purple smoke— "grape" in Army parlance.

"Otherwise, we go in at three o'clock, you from in front, us from behind."

"Squeeze play," Nanos commented. The Greek slapped his hands together in front of him, then flicked a crushed deerfly from the palm of one hand. "Like that," he said and beamed.

Barrabas, Hatton, Nanos and Billy Two followed Jake Larraby into the forest in a single line. For a while, the cowboy picked his way from tree to tree, following no discernible path through the dense vegetation. The going was rough, more so as the ascent became steeper. They stumbled through undergrowth, and swinging branches stung their arms and faces.

Abruptly, Jake stopped, and the mercs crowded around him. They were standing on a narrow trail that led to the top of the mountain. Jake knelt and pointed to a small pile of animal droppings.

"Mostly this trail is used by animals now," he told them. "Deer, rabbits and mountain lions. But I believe it's been used to get to the top of this mountain since the time of the Indians. This valley was sacred to 'em. I've found arrowheads and such now and again when I came up here for hunting.''

"Is that when you saw Doule and the blond man in the photographs?" Barrabas asked.

Larraby nodded. "And that ain't all. They'll have a good number of their men with them, and an equally good number of womenfolk and children. I heard the women are all wives of Doule. Hard to say what's really going on, though. These people don't take kindly to strangers wandering over their property. Couple of times hikers have disappeared after coming into this valley. I joined search parties each time. Never found a trace of them.''

He jerked a thumb in the direction of the top of the mountain. "I got the feeling they knew more about those disappearances than they ever let on.''

After the short rest, the mercs moved on. The going was much easier over the trail, but it wound back and forth up the steep side of the mountain, more than doubling the distance they had to travel. With twenty minutes left before Hayes and O'Toole launched an assault from the front, Barrabas ordered his people to move at double time.

The column of mercenaries broke into a steady jog, with Larraby huffing and panting, but nevertheless keeping up with them. Ten minutes later the path broke through trees and ended abruptly with a two-hundred-foot vertical drop over a sheer precipice. The mountain valley was spread out below. On their left, the side of the mountain rose another twenty feet to the summit.

The last stretch was the most difficult. Grappling onto roots and branches, Larraby and the four mercs pulled themselves up a rock wall that was inclined at an eighty-degree angle. When they burst through the trees and scrub brush that grew along the edge of the summit, they were on a broad plateau. It inclined with a shallow descent to the ranch buildings, the roofs of which were visible five hundred yards away.

A small herd of cattle grazed contentedly nearby. A few of the beasts turned to eye the newcomers, then returned to the task of ruminating the tough grass. Larraby licked his finger and held it in the wind.

"Westerlies," he told them. "We're in luck. They have dogs down there at the ranch house and we're downwind. Otherwise they'd scent us once we got within a few hundred feet and we'd have a fit of growling and barking to contend with."

Barrabas checked the time. They had five minutes. He fingered the flare in his web belt.

"We can stay in the brush that runs along the edge of the mountain until we get up behind the barn," Jake told him.

"Colonel! Over here." It was Lee Hatton, who stood twenty feet off to one side with Billy Two, looking down at something hidden in the high grass next to the tree line.

Barrabas, Larraby and Nanos joined them. A dead cow lay on its side. Its throat had been slashed, and the udder removed with surgical precision. There was no sign of bleeding, or blood.

"Bled dry," Jake intoned matter-of-factly.

"Like that old rancher Cavendish had a few days ago," Barrabas said.

"What in hell is it?" Nanos demanded.

Larraby shrugged. "They been finding these things up and down the Midwest," he told the Greek. "But no one knows."

"Flying saucers," Billy Two intoned. "I read it in a magazine!" he protested when he saw the others eyeing him.

"Sure," Alex said skeptically. "The kind you find in the checkout lines in supermarkets."

"Guess this about proves it's Aryan Nation stuff," Barrabas muttered to Jake. "Since it's on Doule's property. But what in hell—"

Larraby shook his head and interrupted. "I was just telling you what people are saying, Nile." He pointed out a narrow circle of yellowing blighted grass with a radius of ten feet that surrounded the bovine cadaver.

"That circle's part of the pattern. I heard that this kind of thing gives out high readings of radioactivity, too. Whoever or whatever's doing it, I think the answer's more bizarre than anything the Aryan Nation can come up with. And we don't have time to find out."

Larraby motioned for Barrabas and the mercs to follow. Quickly they filtered into the scrub and low forest of twisted pines that ran along the edge of the plateau, and circled around toward their target.

INSIDE THE RANCH HOUSE, Bathsheba Doule sat in a chair in her second-floor bedroom and flipped through the timeworn pages of her Bible. Ten minutes earlier she had had a very bad experience. She still trembled from the moment of terror she'd felt before she ran from the horrible thing in the field near the cattle. The moment she got back to the house she had turned to her refuge, the book that had all the answers.

She glanced quickly at one of her favorite stories, the one where Cain slew Abel and forever bore the mark of the first murder on his dark skin.

"Mud people," the gray-haired matron muttered contemptuously. But today she was not after that lesson. She wanted the book of Revelation, the one that predicted the coming of Armageddon, the great war between the races from which the pure Aryan Nation would emerge victorious.

Eighteen years earlier her husband, Wilbur Doule, Ronald Doule's father, had had a vision as he lay dying from a state trooper's bullets. He had whispered it to Bathsheba with his last breaths, his vision that his infant grandson, Sonny, would lead the soldiers of the Aryan Nation into their last great battle, the great Armageddon predicted by the book of Revelation.

Sonny, she was convinced, was born to greatness. After all, the Bible told her so.

Bathsheba had dedicated her life to raising the boy from childhood to manhood, and she was pleased with the outcome. Now the war was about to begin. The thing out there in the field was so awful it had to be an omen.

She found the passage she was searching for, and exclaimed aloud the first words she laid eyes on.

"'And a great plague shall come upon the earth!'" The apocalyptic words sent jubilant shivers up and down her spine. But that wasn't the part she wanted. She was convinced there had to be something there about cattle bled from the throat, with their udders surgically removed.

Stories and rumors abounded about these horrible things, which had cropped up for years throughout the American Midwest. She knew the ideas, the gossip that went around, even that sometimes her kind of people were being blamed for it. But as far as she was concerned, there was only one explanation. It was the coming of the Beast, and he had arrived there, now.

Downstairs, the telephone rang.

Bathsheba's ears perked up, and she raised her head from the Bible. Footsteps crossed the kitchen and the phone's ring was cut short. It had to be Nora who answered. Muriel was outside with the children. Bathsheba listened closely.

Her daughter-in-law's murmuring voice carried upstairs, but the words were indistinguishable.

Quietly, Bathsheba put the Bible aside and tiptoed to the extension phone in the hallway. Carefully she lifted the phone from its cradle and put it to her ear.

It was Sonny! He was talking with Nora.

In the kitchen, Nora was oblivious to the eavesdropper, but spoke in hushed tones nevertheless.

"Sonny, how are you?"

The young man's voice sounded distant and the line crackled with occasional static bursts. "We're due in Denver in a few more hours," Sonny said. He told her he was calling from a highway oasis in western Oklahoma.

Groomed as an heir to his father's great power—and in his eyes it was real—Sonny had always had a feeling of relative invulnerability. For the first time ever it was wavering.

He was leading forty men in an assault to take a Denver television station. Once they had control, the videotape of their demands would be plugged into a national satellite system for cable TV. It would be broadcast before the authorities knew what was happening. With America held hostage by the threat of a nuclear explosion in a major city, the government would be faced with mass panic and a civil riot. So they would give the Aryan Nation everything they wanted. That included, of course, Sonny's freedom.

It sounded great in theory, but Sonny had a vague feeling his father was playing him for a patsy.

"Are you okay?" Nora asked. "I wish I could get you outta there. What if everything doesn't turn out like it's planned? Where you gonna go then? Prison somewhere?" Then, in a small voice and quickly, she whispered, "Sonny, I love you."

There was a long silence on the other end of the line. Finally Sonny broke it. "I love you, too, Nora. Ever since—"

"Don't, Sonny!" Nora implored, her heart pounding, and she fought something too painful to remember—the day that she, the father's wife, became the son's lover.

Sonny stopped. "When I get back, Nora, we're going to go away together."

"Sonny, don't do it. Ain't there any way I can stop this from happening?" Nora whispered anxiously.

"When I get back, Nora. I promise."

"Sonny, I'll do anything to stop it." Nora felt blood rising to her head, and the steady boom of her heart, the nervous terror that Bathsheba would walk in any minute.

"Nora, I—"

Sonny's voice was cut off. The line had gone dead. Nora looked at the phone and quickly put it back in its cradle.

Bathsheba carefully put the extension phone down and returned to her bedroom, a dark fury brewing deep inside her. She tore madly through her Bible, the onionskin paper crackling with the rapid turning of the pages until she found what she was looking for.

It was the part about an adulterous woman, and how she was stoned to death for her crime. As far as Bathsheba was concerned, other methods were faster—and equally as efficient.

Rising quickly, she opened a drawer in a bureau and reached for a tiny Derringer nestled among white and simple underwear. In her anger, it never occurred to Bathsheba how strange it was that the phone should suddenly go dead like that.

BARRABAS LAY ON HIS STOMACH among the pines, gazing across the field through the sniper scope on the M-16 Jake had brought along. The cross hairs framed the shifting scenes as he scoped out the ranch buildings.

A couple of dogs played in the dusty yard in front of the house. They were good-looking German shepherds but both were tied to stakes. They could run in circles, but not after anyone. There were four vehicles, two 4x4's, an old pickup and an ancient Chevrolet Biscayne.

A ten-foot-wide satellite dish had been erected on a flatbed beside the barn. According to Jake it was the ranch's telephone pickup as well as for pirate television stations. Barrabas covered Jake while the cowboy darted around behind the dish and quietly climbed the metal struts up the back. At the top, his knife flashed in the sunlight, and the cable to the house was cut.

The only human activity seemed to be in one of the buildings, a bunkhouse beyond the main house. A man came out, urinated against the side of another building and went back inside. Each time the door opened the breeze carried the faintest echo of loud voices and laughter from inside.

It didn't look as if they were expecting anyone.

And it was three o'clock—the designated hour. At the bottom of the mountain, Claude Hayes and Liam O'Toole revved the engines of their 4x4's and began the ascent to the ranch.

Barrabas heard a rustle nearby and turned to see Lee Hatton crouch down beside him. "Colonel, we may have trouble," she whispered quickly. "Alex and Billy scouted ahead and almost stumbled across a woman with a bunch of kids."

"Damn!" Barrabas cursed.

"What do we do?"

"Take them. Have the woman keep the kids quiet. We'll leave Billy Two to guard them—at least until they know we're here."

Lee crept quickly back into the forest.

Barrabas squeezed his eye to the scope again and ran it across the ranch. The one thing he couldn't figure out was where Doule, father or son, might be. Or Dr. Young, the missing scientist. All in all, there was neither enough activity nor enough security out there to indicate they were going to find the men they wanted.

Worse, the Aryan Nation fanatics made his job difficult with their communal life-style. He didn't like kids and women getting in his way. On the other hand, he had to admit the strategy was a good one for the opposition. Mixing the innocents in with the bad guys was the kind of cheap trick he expected from the class of citizen he was dealing with.

He waited for Jake to get back before returning to the cover of the pines just as Hatton slipped through the forest.

"We got them," she panted. "Alex and Billy Two have them sitting down. The kids are too scared to talk. It's kind of pathetic."

Quickly, Barrabas and Larraby followed the woman warrior on a path through the pines until they came to a small clearing. Only a few trees and forty feet of grass separated them from the back of the barn. The house was on the other side.

There were six children, all of them below the age of ten or eleven, four of them girls, one an infant, and three of them sucking their thumbs. They huddled in a circle around Muriel. The plain-faced woman sat quietly, wringing her hands in silence and ignoring the children.

"Billy Two!"

The Osage nodded on the other side of the clearing. He felt silly with his double-barreled shotgun loosely aimed in the direction of a bunch of kids, but until any and all opposition was cleaned out, it was the name of the game and the order of the day.

Jake Larraby sauntered over to Barrabas and whispered quietly, "I think we got one of Doule's wives, and his children here. She won't talk, least not without some persuasion."

Barrabas shook his head. "We can't risk it right now. What've we got out there?" Barrabas jerked his head toward the house.

"Bugger all, I'd say. Not much happening. Little sleepy out there."

The mercenary leader nodded. "Still, we came all this way to find out..."

Larraby laughed quietly and slapped Barrabas on the back. "Nile, I told you it was about time we had a little adventure!"

The colonel returned a smile. "So you did, Jake my friend."

Barrabas waved his people forward. Keeping the barn between themselves and the view from the house, they loped across the field to cover behind a rusting tractor at the edge of the yard.

The dogs lay quietly, pooped from the heat and swatting flies with idle flicks of their tails.

The four mercs leapfrogged two at a time across the front of the barn and ducked into the cool shadows just inside the wide double doors. Quickly they checked out the stalls and the loft. The building was empty save for bales of hay and some old cars torn to pieces.

"I'll bet those teeth are sharp," Nanos commented, eyeing the sleepy dogs from inside the barn.

One of them suddenly looked up and sniffed, testing the wind. Its ears rose stiffly. In the distance Barrabas heard the grind of an engine negotiating the steep curving road that led to the ranch.

If everything went the way he hoped, the noise Claude Hayes and Liam O'Toole made driving up the mountain would bring people outside and get their attention. From the barn, he and his people were ready to close the snare from behind.

Barrabas never forgot the axiom of military planning he'd once learned as an officer cadet. Great plans usually last until the moment the battle starts.

Then all hell breaks loose.

He heard a woman scream and simultaneously another man left the cabin across from the house, his hands undoing his fly in preparation for the call of nature. "Hey!" the guard cried, nature forgotten.

Muriel ran around the side of the barn, waving her arms and screaming hysterically, with Billy Two frantically giving chase.

The man in the door of the cabin ducked back inside and emerged with a shotgun just as the Osage pounced, grabbing the screaming woman. The guard lowered his shotgun at Billy Two.

Barrabas raised the M-16 with the sniper scope to his shoulder, centered the cross hairs and fired off a round just as the other man fired. The guard's throat blew apart, flattening him against the door. His shot went wild and struck the woman.

Muriel was tossed through the air like a rag doll, a bullet hole centered just above her ear. Billy Two flew to the ground and rolled sideways to cover against the barn.

Two other men showed their faces in the door to see what was going on.

Barrabas centered the cross hairs again and fired. One man took it between the eyes. The other fled inside. Hastily the bodies were dragged from the doorway and the door slammed. Billy Two scrambled and stumbled in the open door of the barn.

"What could I do?" the Osage shouted, uncharacteristically angry. "Shoot the broad?"

"Alex, Billy, cover for us!" Barrabas shouted. "Let's go!"

Nanos opened with his Uzi on full-auto, just as gunfire erupted from the cabin. He blasted a mag against the two front windows, taking out glass and curtains, and keeping the guards' heads below the level of the sill. When he stopped to change mags, Billy Two picked up the slack with carefully aimed shots from the double barrel.

The mercenary leader ran into the yard with Hatton and Larraby, each firing 3-round bursts against the cabin as they headed for the ranch house.

The dogs leaped into action, stampeding across the yard toward the mercs until their ropes pulled tight and jerked them backward, head over paws. Both beasts swiftly leaped to their feet, and threw themselves onto their hind legs, barking furiously and spraying saliva from their long white teeth.

A stray bullet from the cabin caught one dog in the flank. It yelped painfully, fell and whimpered off to the sidelines, bleeding badly. Barrabas leaped up the steps of the house, Hatton and Larraby close behind him, just as cover fire from the barn slackened and the windows of the cabin exploded with the dispatch of enemy bullets.

The 4x4's burst over the crest at the top of the road, Hayes and O'Toole at the wheels. They roared into the yard, drawing fire from the three mercs running for the ranch house.

The Bronco screeched in a circle in front of the barn, zigzagging wildly and sending up clouds of dust. Claude Hayes braked sharply, cutting off the guards' firing line to Barrabas. Moving cool, the black warrior jumped out on the safe side and hoisted the M-79 to his shoulder.

He pulled the trigger and the thumper popped its load, the recoil wrenching Hayes's shoulder. The missile shot through a smashed window, exploding immediately. Debris flew through the windows.

The opposition in the cabin was no more.

At the house, Barrabas blasted the lock and kicked open the door with one solidly planted kick. The three mercs swung to each side, anticipating enemy fire, but there was nothing.

As suddenly as the firefight had broken out, it stopped. The mountaintop was silent except for the angry snarls of the unwounded dog, which threw itself at them over and over again, each time coming to the end of its rope and tumbling back.

A dark-haired woman, young and pretty, stood nervously in the kitchen before the three mercs. It was Nora. Lee's eyes dropped. Doule's wife stood in a puddle, so terrified she had wet her pants. She breathed rapidly, her hands up with the palms out.

"Please don't shoot me," she begged.

"Where's Doule?" Barrabas demanded. "It's Doule we want."

"Wh—which one? Sonny? Or... or my husband?"

Barrabas and Larraby exchanged glances.

"Don't worry, girl, we aren't going to hurt you," Jake boomed, lowering his rifle and putting on a warm smile to set her at ease. "Now what's your name?"

"N-Nora. I'm Ronald Doule's wife," she stammered, adding quickly, "one of them."

"Is that another of them out there?" Jake gestured out the open door, where Muriel's body lay in the yard.

Nora nodded hesitantly. "And his children."

"Who is this other Doule?" Barrabas demanded, walking close to her.

She flinched as he came near, hunching her shoulders and putting her hands out as if to keep him away. "Sonny?"

"Yeah."

"He's my husband's son. From his first marriage. She's dead a long time now. Sonny is Ronald Doule, Jr." Nora was growing more and more terrified.

"Where is he?" Jake asked her.

"He's gone to Denver. Please. I'll tell you everything. I'll tell you—"

Without warning, the door that opened onto the staircase swung back and banged against the wall.

"Harlot!" Bathsheba Doule screamed in the opening, her eyes wide and the tiny Derringer clasped in her extended hands. She scanned the room with it, and stopped when it was pointing at Nora. Her knuckle whitened against the trigger.

Something flashed quickly through the air, glinting in midflight.

The matriarch froze, and suddenly the handle of a long knife protruded from her chest. She stood for a moment like that, then her gaze dropped downward to have a look. Then she fell like a log, facefirst, the impact with the floor driving the knife even deeper into her bosom. Her body quivered and was still.

Alex Nanos stood at the outside door with his mouth open, staring at Lee Hatton.

"I told you I had been practicing," she told him.

Nanos turned to Barrabas. "I just came to say there's nothing but dog meat in the bunkhouse, and no sign of anyone else around. Claude went to get the little kids in the forest."

Barrabas looked over at Nora. "You gonna tell us where to find him?"

She nodded quickly. "I just want all this craziness to stop."

Jake Larraby pulled over a chair and sat on it backward, the back against his chest. "Well, little lady, time's a-wasting," he said in a slow and friendly tone. "Tell us what's going down, because if Sonny's in Denver, Colorado, then we gotta be moving right fast."

**11**

In Arkansas, Ronald Doule, Sr., twisted uncomfortably in an easy chair in his private quarters deep inside Mount Zoreb. Frequently he found himself glancing at his watch, marking off the time according to Sonny's mission in Denver, Colorado. Nearby, his important visitor sat patiently with his hands clasped in his lap. Methodically, he tapped his index fingers together. The bluish light cast by a television set flickered over their faces with the changing picture.

They were watching the videotape taken by Bill Stead's cameraman in Rock Springs, Wyoming, four days earlier. Barrabas had just finished routing the attack on the television men. The four Aryan Nation punks—Sonny included—fled toward the blue van.

"You know what this means, don't you?" the visitor whined plaintively.

He was a short sinister man with a bony face, dark eyes and hair. His face was deeply scarred, and he sat rigidly in his chair as if his body were wooden.

When Doule didn't answer, the visitor spoke again, with more persistence.

"You do recognize him, don't you? The man with the white hair."

Doule nodded slowly three times.

The visitor stood up. He was lopsided, one shoulder lower than the other, his hip twisted down and to the side, one foot almost perpendicular to the other. He moved two steps closer to Doule, walking with an awkward limp.

He was a man who had used many names in his life, but most people knew him as Karl Heiss. And most people knew Karl Heiss was dead, buried under the rubble of a bombed-out building deep in the Zairian jungle. Barrabas had put him there.

"Yes, I know who it is." Doule spit. His face screwed up in an angry grimace. His voice sank. "I never thought I'd see that bastard again."

His brain worked the memory of almost fifteen years earlier. Doule was smuggling black market army weaponry out of Vietnam in coffins and body bags, while Heiss, a CIA operative and assassin, was moving heroin. They had met during a brief disagreement among some of their cohorts over the use of cadavers. The initial squabble had been transformed into a mutually profitable business agreement. Heiss operated north of Saigon. Doule had a monopoly over the corpses of American soldiers in the Mekong Delta.

And Nile Barrabas, a young colonel and war hero posted at MAC Saigon stumbled onto both their games and put an end to them. Since then, Heiss and Barrabas had crossed paths many times—always as enemies, two sides of the coin of good and evil. On several occasions, Heiss had been left for dead. But Barrabas's nemesis seemed to have the many lives and casual sadism of cats. He survived, but emerged with more and more disfiguring marks and handicaps in memory of his run-ins with Barrabas.

Heiss hobbled slowly toward the door.

"Where are you going?" Doule demanded sharply.

"The charade is over. I have no further reason to stay."

The leader of the Aryan Nation stood, fury and disbelief spreading across his face.

"What do you mean, you're leaving? You are the liaison with our friends in Washington. It was intended that you remain with us for the duration. In case we—"

"*Was* intended," Heiss repeated, emphasizing the past tense. He gestured toward the television set. The screen was now blank. "Your precious son has stirred up a real hornet's nest by tangling with Barrabas. You can deal with the consequences. Not I."

"But he's dead, dammit! Blown to smithereens."

"You and I no longer share a similar agenda," Heiss said slowly. "I know this man. He's too hard to kill. Much too hard for your lightweight son to have been successful."

Before Ronald Doule could reply, the telephone chimed loudly. Doule picked it up. The line was filled with static, and the voice he heard seemed very far away, but he recognized it—like a dull thud in the pit of his stomach. It was the deputy sheriff in Rock Springs. Smithby was a man who had long been an Aryan Nation sympathizer.

Doule listened and hung up without responding. When he turned back to Heiss, his face was pale. "The body at the ranch Sonny destroyed wasn't Barrabas's," the patriarch said numbly. "It was some woman friend of his. The sheriff covered it up until an autopsy was done. The man is still alive." He sat again, nervously, on the edge of his chair.

A trace of a smile tugged at the corners of Heiss's thin lips. "People who owed me—powerful people—pulled the FBI off the case to give your people a chance to move freely," Heiss hissed. "They're not going to be pleased at all—"

"What are you talking about?" Doule stood again abruptly, and shouted, flourishing a clenched fist. "Barrabas isn't here. Everything is going according to plan. There's no reason to think . . ."

Heiss disregarded the man's pleading with the wave of a hand and limped to the door. He opened it, and turned his twisted body to face Doule once more. "Then you don't know this man. I do. He'll stop at nothing. It was a major blunder." Heiss spoke softly, ostentatiously calm and relaxed. "Listen now, believe me later, but at your own peril. The jig is up before it even starts."

Heiss slipped from the room, leaving the leader of the Aryan Nation to ponder his words.

THE SOLDIERS of the Aryan Nation arrived in Denver at sunset.

The cavalcade rolled in on the interstate and rolled off when it became an expressway leading into the heart of the mile-high city. Fifty miles away the peaks of the Rockies, snow-covered and gray, loomed on the western horizon of the sunless sky. The east was dark, the west drawing what remained of shallow twilight.

The WNNW network television station was a modern three-story glass-and-tile building on a wide avenue, floodlit against a parklike setting. Stands of trees massed into a forest beyond the vast parking lot behind the headquarters. Across the avenue was an expansive golf course.

At the wheel of the Jeep, Chuka braked and pulled into the curb just before the driveway. The two trucks slowed behind him until they stopped.

"There it is," Sonny said to the Jeep's other occupants, seeing the target for the first time. There was a field of perfect grass with the single plume of a small fountain in front of it, and a large vertical blue sign displayed the station's call letters, WNNW, in white. On the roof of one windowless wing a monstrously large white satellite dish was pointed to the heavens.

The main entrance was a wall of glass fronting the lobby, with four sets of double glass doors. Inside there was a security desk, and from two hundred feet the security men were clearly visible. There were two of them.

"Old fogies." Chuka laughed cruelly. He turned to face Sonny with a big smile plastered across his face.

Sonny nodded. He knew this part of the plan was going to be easy, seizing the station, securing it with a perimeter and making the broadcast. The hard part was after that. How long would it go on?

Their force, forty-eight men in all, seemed pitifully small to start a revolution—a joke even. But Sonny reminded himself of the lessons of history. The Bolshevik revolution began with the mutiny of sailors on a battleship. And then there were those hilarious guys—Adolf Hitler and a dozen or so boys—who pulled off the Munich "beer hall" putsch that started the rise of Nazi fortunes.

Sonny had no doubts he was on the edge of a monumental history-making event, the apex of his young life, that the moment he had been told to dream about since he was five years old was finally before him. Sonny had repeated the conviction to himself over and over during the long drive from Arkansas, and still he hadn't been able to rid himself of a few lingering doubts.

Spiker leaned forward from the back seat, sticking his head between Sonny and Chuka. "The Field Marshal's on his way—shall we salute or give him the fucking finger?"

Sonny twisted around and glanced out the window. Keith Rotsky trotted over, and leaned down to speak in the window. There was a grim intensity that he deliberately projected, one reason for his nickname. The other reason was his pomposity.

"We're ready to go the moment you are through the front doors," Rotsky said. His voice was low and secretive.

"What are you afraid of, that the streetlights will hear you?" Sonny said casually, pulling a MAC-10 out from under his coat. "We ain't gonna need help. Those old men in there won't know what hit 'em."

"Be ready for anything," Rotsky hissed.

"Heil Hitler," Sonny said, laughing dismissively.

The Field Marshal flushed, his brow furled, but he stopped what he was about to say in anger. Then he spoke in a slow monotone. "Some day you're gonna wish you weren't such a smartass."

Sonny looked at him, surprised—and frightened—by the sudden candor.

With a last withering look, Rotsky straightened and walked back to the cab of the first truck.

Chuka slipped the jeep into gear. "Ready?" he asked Sonny.

Sonny took a deep breath. The moment they went into the station, there was no turning back. Seizing it was a snap. But always the nagging questions. Where would it go? How long would it last?

Sonny nodded.

The jeep moved forward.

NILE BARRABAS and the SOBs picked up Sonny's trail pretty fast.

The woman named Nora at the Doule ranch in Utah told them everything she knew, which was that Sonny was involved in some kind of a takeover of a television station, WNNW in Denver. But it was only as a result of her lover's indiscreet confidences that she knew what little she did, and beyond it, she was in the dark.

It was enough to keep the SOBs on Sonny's tail.

Somewhere over New Jersey, with the lights of Manhattan glimmering through the windows, Jessup received the news of the Utah raid from Barrabas, while aboard the chartered Lear. He told the pilot to turn back to Salt Lake City.

They arrived, badly in need of refueling, and found that the mercs were waiting.

With only the refueling to delay them, it was midevening when they arrived in Denver. As Barrabas descended the steps to the tarmac, city lights twinkled like a carpet of stars, and the summer breezes were warm. It was too perfect for the nightmare unfolding outside a network television station in an office park not far from the downtown core.

At the edge of the tarmac Claymore Jeffries was waiting at the wheel of a Blue Dodge. Another vehicle, a late-model maroon van, was parked behind him. The mercs quickly loaded their equipment into the van and climbed in with Hayes at the wheel. Jessup rode with Jeffries in the Dodge.

Within minutes they were on the expressway leading into Denver.

SONNY, CHUKA AND SPIKER climbed the concrete steps three abreast, tucking their submachine guns under their arms so that they were virtually invisible.

The two security guards at the lobby desk were bent over a newspaper. When the three men reached the top of the steps the guards both looked up. They eyed the young men suspiciously, but made no effort to move.

Sonny, Spiker and Chuka each chose a door and pushed it open. They strode inside.

Sonny moved his arm, revealing the ugly snout of his MAC. Movement in his peripheral vision at each side told him that Spiker and Chuka had done likewise. His finger tightened relentlessly on the trigger.

Suddenly a commanding voice shouted. "Denver Police! You are under arrest! Drop your weapons and lie flat on the floor immediately!"

The words seemed to come from the walls, a sonorous voice, amplified through a loudspeaker. Men in uniforms poured from the corridors that led to the banks of elevators on either side of the security desk, padded and stiff in black fatigues and bulletproof vests.

Then Sonny understood but didn't move. His mouth felt dry and he could barely articulate a thought, let alone words. This was supposed to be the easy part.

Policemen swarmed into the lobby, dozens of them, an arsenal of guns bristling their deadly snouts.

"Drop your weapons!" the amplified voice shouted again, rising a notch in pitch. Two detectives in long coats moved forward, yelling at the three and waving guns, but by this time Sonny couldn't hear. His brain was screaming at him to do something, but he was unable to think.

Spiker's MAC-10 clattered to the floor. He threw his hands into the air, his face frozen in terror. Chuka stiffened, a reaction instantly caught by the wall of police officers. Handguns moved slightly to aim, and the line of executioners opened up, pouring lead just as the punk let off a round from the MAC-10.

The submachine bullet went wild and the gun flew away. Chuka danced like a marionette on a string as police bullets pounded into him from head to foot, jerking his limbs this way and that. Sonny screamed and dropped his weapon. He felt his knees weakening, folding up beneath him, and in panic he threw himself backward through the door.

The wailing of police sirens tore the night to pieces, almost overpowering the roar of truck engines as the two-tons raced up the driveway. Sonny saw red and blue lights strobe along the avenue in front of the station as dozens of police cars converged on WNNW. He dived to the ground and hugged the concrete in an effort to make himself as small a target as possible.

"Attaaaaack!" His righteous call to battle was so loud it pierced the nightmarish clamor.

BARRABAS NOTICED a police car lining up beside the van on the expressway as they hit the outskirts of Denver, then a second police car on the other side.

"Check it out behind us," Hayes said, glancing in the door mirror.

"Looks like they got Jeffries's warning," the colonel commented.

Red, white and blue bar lights on the roofs of police cars flashed over the freeway. More cars poured on from a ramp, stringing themselves across the lanes and merging into the traffic ahead. Then the sirens began, a cacophony of undulating wails that stiffened the air.

Nanos, Hatton, Starfoot, O'Toole and Larraby, divided among the seats in the back, checked mags on their weapons, and packed their pockets with spare ones. A minute later, they followed the blue car off the expressway and turned onto an eight-lane avenue divided down the middle by a boulevard.

Ahead, police cars streamed over the curbs and across the grass, surrounding WNNW-TV. The air was shrill with blasting sirens.

Jeffries kept the Dodge at an even speed, even when he turned off the street into the WNNW's driveway. The two-ton trucks were parked in front of the glass entranceway. Men hopped from the back clutching their rifles at the moment Sonny came fleeing from the lobby.

Rotsky ran from the cab of one of the trucks. The warriors of the Aryan Nation pulled back the olive drab flaps that covered the back of each truck. From behind it, the nasty-looking snouts of two M-60 machine guns pivoted on their tripods and aimed at the Dodge.

Jeffries jinked erratically. The rapid chatter of machine gunfire cut the sirens with its harsh bass beat. The car keeled on two wheels over the curb and onto the grass. The maroon van shot past them, straight toward the trucks forty feet away.

The machine gunner turned the snout of the M-60 on the speeding vehicle and sent a line of fire across the front bumper. Spiderwebs exploded over the windshield.

Claude hit the gas and kicked down the parking brake simultaneously. With an ear-wrenching screech the van skidded into a moonshiner's turn, the back fishtailing in a half circle while the tires kicked out clouds of blue smoke. The entire vehicle spun in a circle, its forward acceleration driving it toward the trucks like a spinning top.

The doors in the back opened and closed, then opened again, flapping wildly on their hinges as the back of the van swung around to face the fire from the Aryan Nation terrorists. Hayes snapped off the parking brake, steering frantically to bring the van out of its 360-degree turn. The smoking wheels caught at the road, regaining traction. The van lurched forward, in retreat from the WNNW building.

Suddenly, a tongue of fire shot from the back of the van like flames from the mouth of a dragon, roaring as it licked across forty feet of asphalt, an inferno of burning chemical death. Louder still was Jake Larraby's long eerie yodel, ringing through the mayhem.

With O'Toole holding the door open, and Billy Two gripping his belt securely in one hand to keep him from falling out, Larraby held Zippo's tanks between his legs and fired the flamethrower across the transports.

Keith Rotsky and a half dozen Aryan soldiers beside the truck were grabbed by the burning wind that wrapped itself around them. They screamed, their clothing, hair and skin consumed instantly.

The tongue of flame ate across the trucks' canvas canopies and enveloped the cabs. Shouts and screams of terror grew frantic, and the tongue kept crawling. Men, human torches, plunged through the fiery canvas like wasps burned from a nest. They ran in crazy circles or rolled on the ground pounding their arms in futile attempts to smother the flames and escape the hot death eating through their bodies.

Once again, the brakes of the mercs' van screeched. It fishtailed wildly and slowed. A man ran from the conflagration and disappeared around the back of the TV building. Barrabas leaped from the cab and spun across the grass, his eyes searching the dark shadows beneath trees and behind shrubbery for the fleeing terrorist.

Barrabas rounded the corner and saw him again, racing toward the wooded forest. The mercenary doubled his speed, running lightly and almost silently across the soft grass, slowly gaining. The fugitive heard his hunter and turned back. Barrabas saw the terrified eyes in light reflected from the TV station. And the blond hair. Sonny Doule.

Barrabas bounded forward, faster, closing in on Sonny just as the young man hit the tree line. The commando

sprang like a puma, hurtling across the space that separated them and in a flying tackle grabbed the man's leg.

Sonny flew head over heels. The two men pounded
against the trunk of a tree. Sonny kicked and squirmed
hysterically, facedown in the mud. Barrabas wrapped his
arms around the youth's legs to restrain them. Sonny
clawed at the ground to pull himself away, but the man
held fast, digging his feet against the tree for leverage and
pulling the young man to him.

The struggle was short. Barrabas soon held him securely in a neck lock, his arm pressing deeply into Sonny's throat. Doule's breathing was a harsh rasp. The
commando pressed the nose of his Browning HP into the
underside of the terrorist's chin, and dragged him from the
forest just as Nanos, Hatton and Billy Two raced across
the grass. Rounding the TV station at a slower pace was
Walker Jessup.

The sirens had stopped, but were quickly replaced by the
distant approach of ambulances. From the other side of
the station, Claymore Jeffries appeared with a host of police officials. He shouted orders, quickly setting up a perimeter to cordon off the area to protect the mercs from
interference.

Barrabas threw Sonny down spread-eagled on the grass,
and kicked his legs farther apart. Quickly he frisked up
and down the man's body, removing a knife, and several
mags for the MAC-10. Inside Doule's fatigue jacket he felt
something hard, and pulled out the videocassette.

The colonel grabbed a handful of Sonny's hair and
pulled his head up to face him. "Is this what you were
supposed to broadcast?" Stepping back, he threw the
black case to Jeffries, who approached behind the mercs.

"My people have one guy," Jeffries told them, catching the cassette. "Says his name is Spiker. Other than that,

everyone's dead from that crazy cowboy's Zippo. And no sign of the bomb."

"We got this one, too," Barrabas snarled, "and he's a real treat." He grabbed Doule by the collar with one hand, anger fueling his strength, and heaved his prisoner to his feet with the gun pressed into his temple.

"We need some information. You're going to give it to us!"

"Fuck you!" Sonny spat in Barrabas's face.

The commando swore tightly between his clenched teeth. He forced Sonny to his knees and with one hand clenching a handful of blond hair yanked his head up and showed him the Browning's muzzle. Terrified eyes stared from close range at a black hole that seemed to stretch all the way to hell. Another frantic glance revealed the skin tightening on Barrabas's knuckles.

"You going to talk to us?" Barrabas shouted.

Sonny Doule nodded yes.

"Where's the bomb?" the commando leader demanded. "And the missing scientist?"

"Arkansas, Mount Zoreb. It's in the Ozarks," he said with something in his voice that sounded close to resignation. He felt cheated, as though he hadn't been fully apprised of the situation and had been misled. "Near Bentonville," he added.

Barrabas shoved him away and looked at Jessup and Jeffries. "There was a place in Arkansas on the list of Aryan Nation safehouses. We were supposed to hit it after Amarillo."

"It's the same," Jeffries nodded. "It's called Mount Zoreb after a small mountain on the property."

"No, it ain't." It was Sonny's petulant voice. Unexpectedly, he spoke, volunteering the information. "It ain't 'cuz o' that. It's where the bomb—" The man paused, weighing his next words. He looked up slyly at the mercs encircling him. "Inside the mountain."

"You mean it's hidden—inside the mountain?" Jessup demanded.

Sonny nodded. "A cave," he said.

Barrabas looked at Jeffries. "Can you get us out of here? With him? Look, once the men back at that compound in Arkansas find out that Denver got screwed up, they're going to kill the scientist if they haven't already. And they'll move the bomb to a safe hiding place."

"What are you proposing?" the FBI agent asked.

"Clamp a media lid on what happened here. We take what weapons we have, leave now and parachute into the compound. And we take him." Barrabas indicated Sonny Doule. "To help us get inside."

Jeffries looked thoughtful. "Keeping the media quiet for that long isn't easy, but I can try."

The mercs closed around Jeffries and the colonel, nodding their agreement.

"Tell them a man's life is at stake—and maybe many lives," Hatton said.

"How'll you get out?" Jeffries demanded, looking from merc to merc.

A smile spread across Alex Nanos's face. "When we're finished with them, we'll just help ourselves to the car pool!"

"Or you can arrange for transportation to meet us there after we're in."

Jeffries nodded. "I can take care of that. And I can probably persuade the Denver police chief to help put the screws on the media, at least for a few hours. But I also have to get back to Washington. I'm disobeying orders as it is by involving myself in this case. I still don't know where that directive came down from, and I have to get to the bottom of it. I have a feeling someone's working behind the scenes for the Aryan Nation's cause. Someone powerful.''

Barrabas hauled Sonny to his feet. "Get up. You're going for a ride."

Sonny looked wan and sickly when Barrabas spoke again. "You're going to get us inside that mountain."

## 12

By midnight, the SOBs were ten thousand feet above the dark valleys of the Ozarks. The night was clear, and a gibbous moon rising in the northeast cast its cold silvery light over the mountains, forests and lakes on the earth below.

The pilot of the chartered jet had agreed to cooperate after a long bout of persuasive arguing by Walker Jessup at Denver airport, supplemented by a substantial bribe. The Fixer's bill was now running close to a million dollars. And the Denver chief of police had persuaded the wire services and television stations to keep the lid on the events in Denver for a total of four hours.

The pilot of the Lear jet navigated by following the inlets of the huge Beaver reservoir, and then used the summit of Swain Mountain, the highest point south of the dam. Mount Zoreb's forested slopes rose to its rocky summit, between lights that marked the villages of Monte Ne and Wareagle.

The compound was on the southern ridge of the mountain, in complete moon shadow unbroken even by house lights. On the southern flank, large open fields ran down to a small river that snaked toward the reservoir. In the cockpit, Barrabas checked his map, and found it was the Wareagle River.

"That's it," Barrabas told the pilot. "Turn and swing back over those open fields at about two thousand feet."

The airman shook his head sorrowfully, still wondering if he was going to end up with his ass fried for breaking every FAA regulation in the law books. On the other hand, it promised to make him fifty thousand tax-free dollars richer. A check, signed by Walker Jessup, was already in his pocket.

Barrabas left the pilot and went back to the cabin, where the other mercs waited quietly. Larraby had stayed in Denver, regretting sincerely that he wasn't born for skydiving and never intended to try it.

Larraby's regret was great, because from the information they had got out of Sonny, the Aryan Nation headquarters was unique. There were five levels in the caverns inside Mount Zoreb, with Young and the bomb on the lowest level, and the scientist's room on the third. Ronald Doule, Sr., had his quarters on the fourth level. Apparently, so secure were the leaders of the Aryan Nation about their hiding place, most of their manpower had been sent to Denver, leaving a light guard of twenty men in the mountain.

Still, the mercs had two problems that Barrabas didn't like. The first was the hike overland from the landing zone to the entrance of the cave. They would be covering unknown difficult territory at night. It was going to take time, and time was at a premium, given the urgency of the situation in view of the kind of people they were dealing with. In a few more hours, the media would start broadcasting news about the death inferno at WNNW in Denver, warning the contingent of Aryan Nation extremists at Mount Zoreb.

The second problem concerned the cave. Inevitably, it was easy enough to get into a place like that. Submachine guns and grenades usually took care of most of the resistance. Equally inevitable, however, was the difficulty in getting out.

In the cabin Lee Hatton and Alex Nanos were going over O'Toole's and Hayes's parachutes. Billy Starfoot stood by the sealed door, one of his great paws firmly gripped around Sonny's arm. The young Aryan Nation warrior looked sickly. Like Jake Larraby, he, too, insisted that he could not skydive. But Sonny had no choice. Barrabas ordered a parachute brought for him, and lashed it securely to the sovereign's back himself.

The pilot brought the airplane around, and the horizon of the earth tilted on a vertical angle outside the plane. The Lear lost altitude quickly, descending over the fields but staying carefully on the north-facing slope of Mount Zoreb, out of view of anyone on the ground at the Aryan Nation compound.

At a signal from the pilot, Hayes unlocked the door and slid it back. At their low altitude there was no depressurization, but strong wind and a loud roar from the slipstream filled the cabin.

Hayes looked at the other mercs with a big smile and abruptly fell backward out the door. His parachute billowed automatically and for a moment he seemed to float. Then, the velocity of his descent arrested, man and parachute gracefully fell to earth.

Alex Nanos was the next one out, exiting with a frenzied scream that died behind him as the Lear's relentless speed left him behind. Lee Hatton followed, then O'Toole, the parachutes floating at different altitudes along the sky like dandelion seeds.

"Billy!" Barrabas called.

The giant Osage moved to the open door, his massive hand still tightly clutched around the sovereign's arm. The young man struggled and protested, but to no avail.

"Your parachute will open automatically. If it doesn't, this is the backup," Barrabas told Sonny, lifting a drawstring from the folds of the parachute strapped to his back. "Pull it to release."

Barrabas grabbed his other arm and nodded at Jessup. He saw the Fixer mouth words that were not audible in the roar of the wind. Barrabas read "Good luck," from the movement of the Texan's lips.

Jessup flattened himself against the wall of the fuselage with one hand clenched tightly to the door handle. Barrabas nodded at Billy Two.

The two men leaped forward with Sonny gripped firmly between them. The prisoner's protests tapered into a scream of terror that fell away as the men descended.

Several seconds after the jump, Barrabas and Billy Two let go of their prisoner. For several more seconds, the mercs and Sonny plummeted like stones. Then, simultaneously, their chutes flowered, cupping the air, and they floated down like hanged men.

Throwing his weight against the door, Jessup slid it closed and sighed with relief when the roar of the slipstream died, and the lock caught securely. He waited a moment to catch his breath, for the first time noticing that his heart was pounding in his chest. Then he made his way forward to the cockpit.

Already the pilot was banking toward the east and turning the plane around.

"New York," Jessup told him.

"New York it is," the pilot confirmed, adding enthusiastically, "with pleasure."

CLAYMORE JEFFRIES ARRIVED in Washington, D.C. at almost the same time the mercs were dangling in the sky over the Ozarks.

As he left the arrivals lounge with the other passengers, briefcase in hand, a dark-haired man in a blue uniform and a peaked hat approached him.

"Mr. Jeffries? Your office sent a car here to pick you up."

For a moment the FBI agent was taken by surprise, but he remembered informing his office of the return time, and was glad for the considerate courtesy. After a week of chasing after the Aryan Nation, he was exhausted.

Outside he had a second surprise when he saw the car was a stretch limo. He wondered briefly whose budget it was coming out of, but once again in his exhaustion he asked no questions and gratefully accepted the luxurious gesture.

The driver climbed in, and a few moments later they were on the parkway that led from Dulles into the capital. The subtle vibrations of the car lulled him into a sleepy state, and without realizing it, he put his back against the comfortable seat and stumbled into a world halfway between dreaming and waking.

Some conscious part that remained told him the car had come to a halt, and he awoke with a start. Momentarily disoriented, Jeffries looked through the tinted window, unable to recognize where he was. A modern business tower set in the center of a granite plaza rose forty stories above, most of the floors in darkness.

"Where are we?" Jeffries demanded sharply. Then he noticed other high-rise buildings and recognized a government office park on the southeastern fringe of Washington.

The driver was silent.

Jeffries rapped on the glass separating him from the driver's seat, and when he still had no response, he looked for and found the button that lowered it.

"Dammit, I asked you where we are!" the fatigued agent shouted over the whine of the window motor.

Finally the chauffeur turned. "To the thirty-eighth floor," he answered slowly. "The meeting you requested. He's waiting."

"Who's waiting? Dammit what's going on here?"

"I was instructed to bring you here from the airport. He said you had requested a meeting."

"Who?"

The driver turned his head and looked at Jeffries with baleful dark eyes. "The man who instructed me to meet you at the airport. You have to get out here."

With that, the driver got out and opened the rear door. Jeffries climbed out and stared up at the tall building. The driver got back in the car. Immediately the limousine eased away from the curb and disappeared down the driveway that led to the street.

Jeffries crossed the broad open plaza, his eyes searching beyond the glass walls of the lobby for signs of security men, but the ground floor of the building appeared empty. The doors were open. He went inside, noticing that there was no sign of anyone, even at the security desk. He noticed the bank of elevators that led to floors twenty-one through forty. He walked past them to a row of pay phones set in a marble cloister.

Quickly, he took out his wallet and removed the card with the telephone number that would connect him to Walker Jessup aboard the chartered jet.

WORKING BY MOONLIGHT, the mercs quickly cut away the ropes that bound them to their parachutes, shucked the straps from their backs and readied their weapons. Barrabas and O'Toole found Sonny Doule before he could extricate himself from the parachute. O'Toole gagged him while Barrabas cut away the chute and tied his hands behind his back.

The mercs moved swiftly to the forest that ran across the slope of Mount Zoreb south of the fields where they landed. Hidden by trees, Hayes squatted and unfolded a topographical map, while Hatton illuminated it with a tiny penlight.

Barrabas knelt beside the black man. Hayes put his finger at a spot on the map.

"We're about here. If we work our way around the mountain laterally at the tree line—and if the information our Aryan Nation friend has given us about this cave is accurate and not some trick to set us up—we should come out directly over the entrance in about a mile."

"Let's do it," Barrabas said curtly, rising to his feet. "Hayes and I'll take point. Starfoot and O'Toole drag. Lee and Alex, stay in the middle with the prisoner. If he tries anything—" Barrabas threw Sonny Doule an icy look "shoot him."

Lee Hatton grabbed the young man's arm and roughly pushed him into line. The mercs started toward the objective.

INSIDE MOUNT ZOREB, Dr. David Young paced in his tiny, windowless room, knowing he had reached a decision but unable to acknowledge it. From time to time he reached deep into his pants pocket and took out his most precious item.

A watch.

It had been lying on the shelf above a sink when he was taken for his daily shower. Someone had taken it off to wash his hands and forgotten it. He had no idea how accurate the time on it was—or even if it was day or night. But for the first time in weeks it provided him with a means of measuring time, of orderly organization that he, as a scientist, craved. And with it, the cogs and gears of logic began to tick away inside his head, presenting him with a solution to the dilemma he confronted.

The more he thought about it, the more he realized it was the only course of action. Nevertheless, it was a difficult decision to make, and he went over it again and again in hopes that he might stumble across another way out.

After several hours, however, he knew he had procrastinated long enough. He pressed a buzzer in the wall by the door. Almost immediately the lock clicked and a guard stuck his head into the room.

"Yeah?" he demanded sullenly.

"I have to make some adjustments to the device," he said, using the same euphemism his captors had begun to use for the nuclear bomb. "Fine-tuning. I'd like to go now."

"Yeah?" the guard said suspiciously. He closed the door without further word, leaving Young alone and in silence.

A few minutes later, the door opened again. "Okay, Doule says you can do it."

The guard stood aside, allowing Young to exit the tiny room.

The prisoner was accompanied to the elevator, which descended and opened into the immense cavern where the laboratory had been built. Half a dozen guards lounged around the corners of the concrete pad, straightening quickly when the doors opened. The cavern was dim with the fluorescent lights off. A single bright spotlight beamed down on the polished artillery shell as if it were a priceless sculpture in an art museum.

Young stood over it, quickly removing the brass plate over the guts of his bomb. Checking the guards with his peripheral vision, he carefully slipped the watch from his pocket and put it inside the shell casing on top of the elaborately wired detonator. With pliers he removed the glass over the face, and quickly clipped several wires inside the bomb.

He worked deftly, attaching the wires to the hands of the watch, hesitating only briefly when he activated the detonating device, priming the bomb to explode.

IT TOOK THE MERCS almost an hour to traverse the mountain, impeded by thick forest, and climbing up and down the sides of a steep gully with a narrow stream in the bottom. Finally the forest opened on a ledge that commanded a view of the southern slopes of Mount Zoreb. A farmhouse, its windows dark, stood at the crest of a hill half a mile away.

In the moonlight, Barrabas made out a narrow slash of a road weaving in and out between the trees and up the slopes of the mountain to the limestone wall below them. Barrabas lowered himself to the ground and elbow-walked to the edge of the precipice. There was an eighty-foot drop straight down. The rutted gravel tracks of the road appeared to end in a stone wall below.

"Now what?"

Barrabas looked sideways to see Claude Hayes on his belly beside him. "We have enough rope to rappel down there?" the colonel asked.

"Not unless we go back for the parachutes and tie them together," he suggested.

Barrabas shook his head. "It'd take too long. We'll have to walk around the side of the mountain until we find a way down."

Twenty feet away, Billy Two squatted and picked up a small pellet from a place where the grass had been flattened. Rabbit dung. Looking carefully, he followed stems of grass that were flattened or broken to the back of the precipice. There, poking among trees and underbrush, he found an animal trail that led to a narrow ledge running several hundred feet across the limestone cliffs. On the other side, a generous slope would allow them to descend quickly. Below it was a quick fall to death.

The trail they'd followed to the Utah ranch could be used by men or even burros, but traffic on this one was strictly small mammals. Starfoot wondered for a moment if it would support a grizzly-bear-sized Osage Indian. He shrugged and turned, seeing Nanos walk up behind him.

"There is a way down here," he told the Greek softly. Alex heard the Osage mutter something else, but couldn't make out the words.

"Hawk Spirit, don't fail me now," Billy Two said under his breath, stepping out onto the narrow ledge.

Barely a third of his foot fit on it, so he dropped his weight onto the ball of each foot. With his bare fingers clawing into crevices in the rock, he began tiptoeing to the other side. Nanos watched from the sideline. Once he glanced over the edge to see the drop. When he did, his heart dropped into his stomach and he stood back, averting his eyes.

O'Toole ran up and was about to speak when Nanos pointed. The Irishman saw the dark figure of the Osage creeping along the rock wall, already halfway to the other side.

"Good Lord!" he exclaimed. He waved to the other mercs, and they swiftly drew close, Hayes pulling Sonny along with him.

"Colonel, I think our loony Indian friend has found us a way in," he told Barrabas.

"Is that right, Sonny?" Barrabas demanded.

The gagged man nodded. The mercs watched Billy Two step off the ledge onto the other side.

"Who's next?" Hayes asked.

Nanos gulped, and stepped out.

It took twenty minutes to get everyone across. Sonny's bonds were removed. Ordered to cross, he made it halfway and froze in stark terror. Eventually Barrabas and Billy crept out to him on either side. Gripping the trembling man by his arms with one hand and clutching the rough surface of the rock with the other, gradually they forced him across. Hayes was the last over.

Barrabas glanced at his chronometer and swore softly.

"What's up, Colonel?" Lee Hatton asked.

"Our four hours of media silence in Denver is up in ten minutes. If that news gets out, this will cease to be a surprise attack, if you know what I mean."

Hatton nodded. She did.

"Tie up the prisoner again and let's move out," Barrabas commanded.

For a while the animal trail continued, but it suddenly seemed to end abruptly, and Barrabas led the mercs down through the fir trees and oaks that grew on the slopes. The road appeared and disappeared through the forest as they descended, but he was able to use it as a navigational aid, heading to the point where it seemed to join the mountain.

Finally the mercs walked onto a wide grassy ledge twenty feet above the road. Moving with exquisite silence, Barrabas and Hayes once again crept forward to reconnoiter. The cleft in the rock that led to the caverns was clearly visible from above. Four guards sauntered about below, obviously bored and not bothering with a great show of alertness. One was furtively smoking a cigarette.

The mercs moved away and huddled with the others.

Barrabas heard Sonny whimper through his gag and swung around to face the young man. Gripping his Browning, he jammed the barrel against the young man's temple.

"You make a goddamn noise, you're dead," he said in a very low and savage voice. "Got it?"

Sonny nodded.

Carefully, Barrabas loosened the gag.

"Is there a way down from here?" he demanded.

Sonny pointed to the other side of the ledge, where the limestone cliffs were staggered and broken in a descent to the road. "There," he whispered hoarsely.

"Lee, check it out."

"How far down is it if we jump?" Nanos asked.

"Fifteen, twenty feet," said Barrabas. "There are four guards and they looked bored and tired."

"We'll jump them?"

The colonel nodded as Lee returned to the huddle. "We can get down that way."

Barrabas turned to the others. "Billy, Claude, Liam, we'll jump first and go one to a man. If we drop on top of them, it'll cushion the fall. Alex and Lee, stay with the prisoner and go down the other way while we secure the cave entrance."

Wordlessly, the mercs moved into position hunched like great gargoyles at the rim of the ledge, each positioned directly above a guard. Barrabas signaled with his hand.

Simultaneously they dropped.

Starfoot and Barrabas hit first, their boots driving into the guards' shoulders and throwing them down. They were dragged aside and knocked unconscious.

Claude Hayes dropped directly behind the third guard, and with a hard and swift blow made sure he wouldn't interfere for the next hour.

O'Toole grabbed his man's head as he landed, pulling him down and rolling across the stony ground. The guard broke free, and jumped. Starfoot saw the escape attempt just as O'Toole threw himself forward and grabbed the guard's ankle, tripping him. The man fell on his face.

Starfoot took over and swiftly bound and gagged him. The guard squirmed in protest, but subsided after receiving a tap on his head.

Hatton and Nanos ran along the road, pushing the bound and gagged prisoner between them. Barrabas grabbed him, jamming the handgun against his neck.

"This is the part where we need you. Afterward, you're expendable, understand?"

Sonny nodded.

"You'll live as long as you don't screw up. If you do, your life's worth shit, got it?" He cocked his pistol.

Sonny nodded even harder.

Barrabas removed the gag and pushed Sonny ahead of him into the cleft of Mount Zoreb.

The steel door was unattended, and barely distinguishable in the dim light of a single industrial light fixture. Barrabas spotted the video camera, and used Sonny as a shield, angling carefully so as not to be spotted. He kept his weapon pressed against Sonny.

"You blow it, this gun is going to take your miserable life—and not in a quick and easy way, either."

Sonny swallowed. He pressed his hand against a stainless steel pad beside the door. A red light on the pad blinked, and a voice barked from an intercom, demanding identification.

"Sonny Doule. Bones in, bones out."

The video camera whined, swinging toward the young man. After a short pause, the voice announced, "Clear to enter." The steel door rolled back with a quiet sigh.

They walked into the first cavern, where cement had been poured for the floor, and the walls were white-washed and brightly lit. Several huge fuel tanks lined one wall, and half a dozen assorted 4x4s and Jeeps were parked along the other. At the end, there was the elevator. Barrabas waved his gun and the mercs quickly fanned out to take stock of the room.

A few moments later O'Toole announced a locked door behind the fuel tanks.

"A fire exit," Sonny told them. "It's never used."

The elevator doors slid open, and Lee Hatton stood in the door to hold it.

"Liam, I want you to plant explosives under the fuel tank. Lee, stay with him. Move one of those 4x4's out of here and keep the entrance secure. Alex, Billy, Claude, come with me."

The four mercs entered the elevator, pushing Sonny in with them. Barrabas pressed five, the doors closed and the car descended. The mercs braced themselves in the tiny moment after the elevator stopped, waiting for the doors to slide back.

The cavern was immense, with awesome stalactites suspended like stone icicles from the ceiling. The laboratory was ahead of them, the bomb bathed in amber light from the overhead spot, the artillery shell gleaming like a polished brass phallus.

Two guards shared a cigarette and a joke nearby. One looked over casually when he saw the light over the elevator come on. The four mercs walked out. It took the guard a second to realize he didn't know them.

"Hey!" he swung around, leveling the Aryan Nation favorite, a MAC-10.

Hayes and Nanos braced their legs and fired. Uzi rounds tore into both men, zipping blood lines across their bodies. The mercs left Hayes to guard Sonny and fanned into the cavern, searching for the scientist and more of the enemy.

The cavern was empty. The mercs approached the laboratory area, walking quietly around the bomb. Billy Two leaned over it, pressing his ear to the metal. He looked up at the other mercs.

"It's ticking!"

The men exchanged glances. Barrabas pressed his ear to it. The Osage wasn't having auditory hallucinations. Very faintly in the metal casing he heard the regular tick of a timing mechanism.

"Jesus Christ!" Barrabas cursed, his voice almost a whisper. "Let's get the hell out of here."

They ran back to the elevator. Barrabas grabbed Sonny by the throat and slammed him against the wall.

"Young's not here. Now goddammit, take us to him."

"On three," the prisoner gurgled, fighting to breathe.

Barrabas released him. The doors closed and the elevator ascended.

On three, the doors opened onto a long sterile corridor. Two guards on either side of the closed door glanced at them. Their eyes registered surprise at the mercs' faces, but it was already too late.

Barrabas's and Nanos's Uzis sang their lead hymn. The impact of the bullets smashed the two men against the wall, red spattering across the pristine white expanses. They slid to the floor, blood tracks running down the wall behind them.

Barrabas ran forward and tried the door. It was locked. Billy Two moved in beside him, and fired his double-barreled shotgun once. A sizable section of the door blew into fragments. Barrabas kicked it open.

David Young, the missing scientist found at last, backed against the wall, his face white with terror.

"We're your rescuers!" Barrabas shouted, grabbing the man by the arm and pulling him forward.

There was a yell in the hallway, and the mercs rushed out to see Claude Hayes doubled over in pain and the elevator doors closing on Sonny Doule.

"He kneed me," Hayes groaned painfully.

"The stairs!" Barrabas shouted. He turned to Young. "You know where they are."

The timid scientist shook his head. Then he grabbed Barrabas's wrist and looked at his chronometer. "We don't have time to get out," he told the mercs. "I timed the bomb to detonate."

"You what?"

"They were going to use it on a city. I rigged it to blow up here and destroy everything. Them, this mountain. Me," he added quietly.

"How long do we have?" Barrabas demanded.

Young shrugged. "There's no way of knowing because obviously your watch wasn't synchronized with the one I used. Five, ten minutes."

Suddenly, from speakers hidden in the ceiling, a piercing alarm sounded a long steady wail.

IN HIS QUARTERS on the fourth level, Ronald Doule, Sr., was getting edgy. First the contact from Washington had bailed out, and still he had no word from Denver. In a corner, the television blared a satellite broadcast from an all-news network.

"And this just in from Denver," the anchorman began.

Doule pointed the remote and turned up the volume.

"A terrorist attack on WNNW television was foiled in the late hours before midnight when—"

Doule stopped listening. A camera panned over the charred remains of the trucks. Men in white clothes wheeled stretchers with body bags.

He swallowed nervously, hands tightening around the MAC-10 he carried, feeling the unmistakable clutch of failure in his gut.

Then his solitude was interrupted by the relentless peal of the emergency alarm.

THE MOMENT the elevator doors closed, Sonny pressed the alarm button. A moment later, the doors opened onto the fourth level. Doors slammed and men rushed past him, clenching rifles and shouting wildly. Doule, Sr., ran up the corridor and met Sonny at the elevator. He looked as if he was seeing a ghost.

"The bomb's been armed," Sonny shouted at the top of his lungs, his voice carrying over the tumult. "It's going to go off!"

Like the sudden silence in the eye of a hurricane, there was a moment where everyone stopped, and then the hurricane began anew, with panicking men clawing at one another to get out of the mountain.

Doule lowered the ugly snout of his MAC-10 and opened up. He blew the whole mag back and forth across the corridor, shooting his own men in the back. They tumbled, fell, tripping and stomping over one another, the tight mass of fleeing men lubricated by their own gushing blood. The surviving men retreated to the far end of the corridor and opened fire just as Doule, Sr., jumped into the elevator with Sonny and three others.

The doors slid closed and began to ascend.

"COLONEL!" Billy Two shouted from the far end of the corridor. "I found it. The stairs that go up."

The mercs raced to the end of the corridor where the Osage held open a door. The metal stairs were circular and seem to stretch up and down indefinitely. Because of the differing heights of the caverns at each level, the exit doors were not spaced evenly.

As the mercs rushed upward, they heard noise echoing from far below, the shouts of men and boots storming up the stairs from the fourth level.

"Looks like we got company," Hayes murmured, stopping long enough to pull a grenade from his pocket. He bit off the pin and dropped it. The explosion left screams in its wake, and for a moment silence. Then the survivors' stampede continued anew.

The mercs ran faster, panting as they climbed in dizzy circles up the staircase. Giant stalactites hung next to the metal steps, and the entrances of other caverns were great dark holes in the rock walls around them. At one point, the steps rose through an opening blasted into the rock ceiling, leading to yet another cavern.

Barrabas turned a curve and spotted the door leading to the second level just as it opened. Several men ran through. Barrabas and Nanos squeezed the triggers of their submachine guns, cutting them down before they made it to the steps.

Young stopped, clutching a railing and holding his hand to his chest, desperate for breath. Billy Two swooped down, lifting him effortlessly off his feet and throwing him over his shoulder. Hayes threw another grenade, then a third over the edge. Again screams followed the explosions, and the storm troopers of the Aryan Nation fell behind for a few moments.

The mercs scrambled over the bodies on the stairs and raced up three more flights to the exit to the first level. They burst into the first cavern where O'Toole unrolled detonating cord across the floor. It spread in every direction like a spiderweb to each corner and several places along the fuel tank. Hatton stood guard at the door out of the mountain. She had a Jeep waiting for the mercs on the road outside.

Barrabas glanced toward the elevator. The number three blinked off, and two lit up.

He leveled his Uzi at the control and blasted it away. The elevator stopped, stuck somewhere between the second and third levels.

"Ready?" Barrabas snapped at O'Toole.

The Irishman nodded.

"Do it!"

O'Toole set the timer for thirty seconds.

The mercs fled the cavern, closing the thick steel door behind them, and running quickly out of the mountain. There was silence as they piled into the Jeep, as though all of them were concentrating very hard in a magical effort to make the vehicle fly from the place.

They were speeding along, well on their way, when they heard the muffled explosion of the plastics inside the cave. It was followed by the nuclear bomb.

Suddenly they were lifted up and coasted along in the air. When the Jeep landed, the earth trembled beneath them. The mountain heaved and tilted, shuddering with violent spasms, and there was a thundering as cavern walls deep underground collapsed, burned and, along with Doule, father and son, were blown to radioactive isotopes of common molecules.

When the ground was calm, some minutes later, they all looked at one another in silent awe. Then all eyes turned toward Dr. Young. He looked just as shaken as the rest of them.

"I wouldn't be too wrong if I hazarded a guess that you've solved the problem of what to do with the bomb they built," O'Toole said at last.

The colonel nodded. "Before we arrived Dr. Young set the bomb to go off." He turned to the diminutive scientist. "It was a brave thing to do."

"I couldn't let them use it to kill millions of people, or even threaten it. It would've meant my hands were dirty, using science for such twisted ends. Even though no one would have known what I had done."

"Just like us," Barrabas commented quietly. His mind swiftly recapped the last week of his life, touched briefly on the memory of Doris Amberton. Then he put it away, another bit of emotional baggage he didn't want to carry with him. There was too much sorrow involved, and it all could handicap him at crucial moments. He had to always settle the past, put things into perspective, so he could carry on, live the lone vengeance of his own singular justice.

"Thank you for coming for me," Young said quietly. "By the way, who are you?"

From the jeep, Alex Nanos, Lee Hatton, Claude Hayes, Billy Starfoot and Liam O'Toole cried in unison, "The soldiers of Barrabas!"

Young looked up at the mercenary leader. "Who?"

Barrabas laughed.

"Sons of bitches," Nanos shouted. "The meanest ones around."

"And you?"

The big man smiled. "I'm Barrabas. Nile Barrabas. And those are the SOBs."

THE MOMENT Walker Jessup heard from Jeffries, he ordered the weary pilot to divert the Lear from New York to D.C. Just before he landed, Barrabas had called from somewhere in Arkansas. They had the scientist, and the bomb was no longer a threat.

But somehow, Jessup didn't think the conspiracy had been ended. And he knew Jeffries didn't, either. Somewhere in the Washington bureaucracy, the Aryan Nation had some powerful people working for them—powerful enough to have the FBI and the SOBs taken off the assignment at one point.

When Jeffries contacted him several hours earlier, he had discouraged the FBI agent from continuing until he arrived. With the defeat in Arkansas and the recovery of the scientist, the extremist organization had been routed. But whoever worked for them in D.C. was still extremely dangerous.

A taxi took him from the airport to the office tower just as the first bare light of dawn broke in the east. A news bulletin on the radio announced that an unexpected earthquake with an epicenter in the Ozarks hit 5.2 on the Richter scale.

"You want me to stick around?" the taxidriver asked as Jessup forked over a twenty. The Fixer looked at the empty plaza. He was alone.

"Nah. I'll call if I need you."

He watched the car drive off before turning to cross the plaza. He squared his shoulders and had just started for the front doors when he heard a strange noise above him. He looked up in time to see a dark object hurtling from one of the windows near the top floor.

Almost immediately, giant pieces of plate glass hit the granite plaza, shattering into millions of pieces. Then an object like a sack of old clothes thudded against the ground. Jessup picked up speed, but he knew what he would find well before he got there.

Whether Jeffries had been alive or dead before he sailed through the window, Jessup didn't know. He was definitely dead when he hit the ground, however. The FBI agent had landed facefirst. Blood slowly spread out from around the body.

Jessup reached inside his jacket and took out his gun.

Strangely, the doors were open but the lobby was devoid even of security guards. He found the elevator, entered and pressed the button for the thirty-eighth floor.

When it stopped, he stepped out.

The corridor ran the length of the building with offices on both sides. At the far end to his left, he heard something banging. When he looked, he saw a door flapping open and shut in the wind.

Carefully, listening for telltale sounds of another person and gripping his handgun tightly, the Fixer walked on. The door ahead of him slammed shut, and for a moment stayed that way. Jessup was about to push it open when it was flung back on its hinges.

The room was bare, unused. All that remained of the plate-glass window was jagged shards of glass. The wind gusted in, invading like an uninvited guest. Invisibly it snaked through the room, flinging the door open and closed. For a moment, Jessup thought it was snowing in the room, which was impossible in summertime. Then he realized it was confetti.

There was a machine on the desk, clicking and humming.

Jessup walked over to it slowly.

It was a paper shredder. On the other side of the desk the wind blew the tiny shreds of paper from a basket, swirling them around the room.

No one had to tell him that the shredded documents contained whatever evidence had existed of a connection between someone powerful, and Ronald Doule and the Aryan Nation. The message was clear.

And it *was* a message.

Whoever left it had taken care of Jeffries for finding out too much. And now they were taunting him. And warning him.

Jessup sighed. Evil was always an unfinished story. And as long as it was, he was thankful for one thing. A man named Nile Barrabas. Nile Barrabas and the SOBs.

From Europe to Africa, the Executioner stalks his elusive enemy—a
cartel of ruthless men who might prove too powerful to defeat.

### DON PENDLETON's
# MACK BOLAN

# Moving Target

One of America's most powerful corporations is reaping huge
profits by dealing in arms with anyone who can pay the price.
Dogged by assassins, Mack Bolan follows his only lead fast and
hard—and becomes caught up in a power struggle that might be
his last.

---